Betrayal's Dust

By

Vina St.Fran

I0669587

Betrayal's Dust

Amorous Trilogy, Volume 2

Vina St. Fran

Published by Zam Publishing LLC., 2015.

First published by Zam Publishing, LLC.

30835 W. 10 Mile Road #4006, Farmington Hills, MI 48336

BETRAYAL'S DUST: the Amorous Trilogy

Layout by Penoaks Publishing, http://penoaks.com[1]

BETRAYAL'S DUST

First edition. November 11, 2015.

ISBN: 978-0996139434

Written by Vina St. Fran.

Dedication

I dedicate this book to my dad, Manuel George Roberts III, a courageous man with a booming voice, and big heart. Thank you for caring and sharing your life with us. You will never be forgotten.

Acknowledgements

First of all, I must thank God for blessing me with the creative gift of writing. It is hard work, and at times, a lonely space that cannot be filled by anything other than the beginning, middle, and the end of a story. Therefore, I am so appreciative of my fans, friends, and family that support me throughout my artistic journey. I don't take you for granted, and remain grateful for your encouragement. A special shout out to my older sister, Hope! Mother Lori Hannah Ruth, you are perhaps one of the best people that I've known in this lifetime, and that's saying a lot! Thanks for everything! Dawn Jones, my BFF (Best Friend Forever), I know I can count on you day or night for anything! Alice Buckley, a woman who has a strong moral compass that in today's times is much appreciated as is your friendship! I am grateful you are just a phone call away.

I need to also express gratitude for my team that makes it happen once I've finished creating the magic including my web designer, Ardnese Payne, book cover designer, Clarise Tan and my PR team. Mucho gracias'! To my amazing editor, Tessa Shapcott, you are awesome and as I've told you many times, it has been such an honor working with you on this exciting project!

Dearest nephew Robert, continue to study hard, so you can play hard later, or I am coming after you! Lastly, to my son Zachary, life is limitless. It is enlightening and refreshing to see you embrace it and grow into an incredible young man. I am forever blessed because of you.

Chapter One

It was impossible to ignore the smoldering heat of the beaming Jamaican sun as beads of sweat formed on Tavie's body. There was so much perspiration, it caused her to wonder if she was going into peri-menopause!

In an instant, Tavie felt the coolness of a lemon-scented towel placed around her neck from behind, as Orville began to aid his woman in beating the heat.

"Dat feel good, babe?" Orville inquired, while rubbing her relaxed shoulders.

"Indeed, it does. I hope you have a cooler of these things because I am literally a hot mess!"

"A couple more days, mon, and it's back to the D."

Tavie felt Orville inhaling the nape of her floral-scented neck. The playful temptress ducked away from him as he teased her that Caribbean women could out-fuck any women in the world. She thought perhaps he might have a point, but she truly didn't care as he went out to play croquet. Tavie's vagina felt as dry and parched as the desert heat of the island, and she doubted her coochie would muster up an ounce of wetness, even if she got aroused.

Orville had whisked Tavie away to an all-inclusive resort for a couple of days as an excursion to give them a chance to have a bit of privacy from his boisterous family and to enjoy other parts of the island. She liked seeing the camaraderie of his family, in that she felt she was becoming a part of it. On the other hand, she believed she was being sized up to see how much she fared against that ex-wife- slut of his, Geneva!

There wasn't an ounce of decency in that bitch, Tavie thought with disgust. Geneva had openly flaunted the affair she'd had going on with Tavie's former boyfriend, Mack, though it had remained unbeknown to Tavie until that fateful rainy night in Lansing. She blamed that train wreck of a whore for the miscarriage she'd suffered.

The irony of how she came to know Orville—she'd had a brief sexual dalliance with him before finding out he'd been *married to* Geneva, her arch-nemesis!—seemed unbelievable to everyone around her. She'd even caught him watching the sex tape with Geneva which he and Tavie had made as foreplay, when she'd unexpectedly showed up at his house, which is how she'd found out about the truth—standing in shock, peeking inside of his living room bay window.

Orville and Tavie were labeled the 'accidental couple' by most of their friends, the reason being that initially it had been about revenge for Tavie after she'd found out Geneva's marriage to Orville. It was game on for her. Mack had tried his damnedest to patch up what was left of them, but it had been too little, too late. A part of her had felt guilty, because Mack had put himself out there for the brief time she'd tried to reconcile with him, only to find herself seduced by Orville. For once in her life she had love, but it didn't intoxicate her.

Jamaica was definitely a haven for lovers. Couples from all over the world could be found making out on most of the nine-mile, pristine beach in Negril. She and Orville got caught up, and Tavie had her first beach orgasm which thrilled her lover.

Tavie loved sex, but she had a more traditional attitude when it came to adventure. She wasn't comfortable with public displays of affection, let alone getting fucked on a remote part of a beach. Cyndarella had told her she needed to try it at least once, regardless of the hours it took to get the sand out of her hair. She was certainly glad she had listened to her dear friend, who in her opinion was the ultimate sexual connoisseur.

The temperature had been in the nineties for most of the two weeks that they had been on the island. Island life had a tempo of its own with its laid back culture. Music and dancing were in abundance, as were the local and tourist stoners, including Orville who stayed high while on vacation.

Tavie gave up smoking cigarettes and had never experimented with weed because of her asthma. Besides, she hated the way it smelled. She'd grown up in a house with her mother who was a chain smoker. Cigarettes stank! Even the little Capri ones she used to puff on. The sweet pungent fragrance of weed had even managed to permeate Orville's dreadlocks, and that had prompted Tavie to pretend she had an allergic reaction to it, causing him to promise to cut his trademark locks when they returned home. The Good Lord knew she'd treasure that day!

Chapter Two

Thinking of homemade Tavie even more anxious to return. This two-week holiday was the longest trip she'd ever taken with a man. Orville was from Port Antonio where he had spent a lot of time growing up and he'd persuaded her he could show her cultural things about the island that only most natives were privy to. He promised her she'd enjoy it, furthermore enticing her by selling it as history she could share with her students. She was sold.

Tavie thought back on the moment the plane had landed at the small but crowded Montego Bay Airport twelve days ago. The heat of the sun and the smiles of the Jamaican people immediately warmed her heart. Orville's Uncle Waldon picked them up promptly, leaving little time for them to be bum-rushed by the mobs of timeshare sales representatives looking for tourists to sell packages to. Tavie was glad, because she'd once fallen for one of those sales pitches in Punta Cana, and what was supposed to be a three-hour presentation had turned into almost an half a day!

Uncle Waldon was very warm and friendly, and joked that Tavie should make sure her seat was buckled for the hour-long drive to St. Anne's, which was right outside of Ocho Rios. Tavie had forgotten that the Caribbean islanders were different to people in the US and drove on the left hand side of the road, and it took all she had not to have a panic attack for the duration of their drive. Reggae music blasting from the stereo made the journey a bit more enjoyable, along with the laughter they exchanged between them. Uncle Waldon had a cooler full of the popular Red Stripe beer for them to consume on their road trip.

Uncle Waldon seemed to know everyone on the road. He honked at everyone he passed, and if he didn't, it seemed someone was honking at him. All of that before they finally reached their current destination, a former Jamaican plantation which was a staple in Orville's family for fun, family, and intoxication.

"So Geneva had a baby?" Uncle Waldon said with laughter in his voice. "You gave her everything but the bun in the oven, she told us".

"She does have a point. I'll give her dat, Uncle. No worries, or regrets, thanks to me lady, Tavie. Right, dear?" Orville gently prodded his lover, drawing her in the conversation.

"Right, lover, right," Tavie sarcastically agreed.

Orville needed everything to go right on this vacation. He'd warned his family ahead of time that he was bringing Tavie, and that they needed to tone down the wisecracking jokes about him and Geneva. Tavie was extremely insecure and insanely jealous about his former marriage and his ex, Geneva, although he didn't admit it to them.

The relationship between the women was frosty, to say the least. Each despised the other, although Geneva loved getting under Tavie's skin and, on several occasions, they'd almost come to blows. It had taken some time, but everything had finally calmed down and Orville did not want to go down that road with her again, which would be good for them both. He had no reason to, really. Nothing tied him to Geneva anymore, especially now, since she'd had a child.

Chapter Three

Cyndarella marveled at the expansive homes in the luxurious subdivision of Clymouth Creek as she drove upon her winding driveway. The Bazzi estate sat on two acres in a stunning setting. The stately new-construction residence had proven to be a labor of love and a pain in her ass because of going back and forth with the builder.

The finished product was definitely worth the wait, Cyn thought. It felt good coming home to something that was custom built for their family. Bashar had made sure everything was as contracted, especially those pesky little upgrades that added up to more than she wanted to think about.

The two story foyer, with its split staircase that included solid oak and wrought iron spindles, seemed to be everyone's favorite. But tonight Cyn was almost too tired to even want to make it up the stairs which led to double doors that opened onto their lavish bedroom and included a den. The loud sound of snoring lured the tired woman down the hall to Nadia's bedroom. While making sure her daughter was nestled in for the night, Cyn could not believe such noise could come from a kid of Nadia's age—she'd just turned seven!

Cyndarella had to refrain from kissing her daughter goodnight because she was such a light sleeper and had just got over the stomach flu. If she did wake her, Cyn knew it would be an invitation to disaster, because Nadia had a hard time falling asleep and tonight she was not in the mood to deal with any of her daughter's nonstop chatter, she thought, as she tiptoed out of her room.

Cyn walked into her bedroom to find Bashar asleep along with their two-year-old identical twins, Zaid and Zahir. One son was laid on the left and the other the right. She had gone to another political meeting for the Democratic Party in Oakland County, which Bashar normally would have accompanied her to. However, the twins were also sick with the stomach virus and he'd decided to stay home with them. Cyn quietly stood at the door, admiring the sight of her good looking family momentarily.

It had been quite a week with work, family and meetings, which was the norm in the Bazzi household. Bashar's career as an international hotel broker meant he closed deals all over the world. But thanks to today's technology he was able to make most of the deals from home, albeit sometimes working around the clock depending on the time zone. It made him tired on many occasions, though he never complained about it. *She* complained enough for the two of them!

Cyn got into the shower and immediately was seduced by the steam that enveloped her senses. As she breathed in the warm vapors, water pellets popped off her body. It had been three days since she'd made love with her husband, and though she had pleasured herself, as a couple they had a five-day maximum rule for going without sex—but they never made it to five. Even with their three kids, they always found a way to get it on.

Tonight's sleepwear decision had been an easy one, Cyn thought, as she slipped into her silk champagne-colored two-piece pajama set. She loved the fitted flair and designs of Julianna Rae's lingerie. She could go from homemaker to hooker with her favorite lingerie designer's nightwear in an instant, and she needed this spontaneity because the reality was that was how she and her hubby rolled, more often than not.

Bashar and the twins weren't in bed when Cyndarella returned from her shower. She hoped their sons weren't hit with a diarrhea or vomiting spell again, as she pulled back the sheets and proceeded to climb in bed and lay her head down on a pillow. She'd tended to the twins for the last three days and given them meds prescribed from their doctor with lots of water so they did not get dehydrated. But tonight, their father would have to care for them; assuredly, she was whipped and needed a break.

The Bazzis' bed had become the family bed since the arrival of their children. Sick days, bedtime stories, storms, or the rare bad dream would send the kids into their room. Nadia had outgrown most of her nightmares, but an occasional fever or thunderstorm sent her right into her parent's bed. Cyn never went to sleep without her Breath Assure mints; they would dissolve as she slept, and she'd trained her husband to do the same.

Chapter Four

"Hell, no," Bashar whispered to himself at the sight of seeing his wife sleeping soundly in their bed. But not for long if he'd had his way. Bashar had been hot and bothered all day after watching Cyndarella this morning dressing for work in a simple pencil black skirt, white V-neck blouse and several layers of the white pearls that he'd gifted her.

She'd quickly slid on her pantyhose and finished the look with red high heel shoes which screamed to him, *Fuck me*! Afterwards, she'd kissed him goodbye and seductively walked away, leaving him with a hard-on and thinking about her all day. He swore she'd pay for that one and had warned her via text, and she'd shot back at him, "*Talk is cheap!*"

Bashar began unbuttoning her silk pajama top, exposing honey-colored bare breasts that stared back at him. Cyn's body was a banquet that he never got tired of feasting on, and sexually neither of them had a limit when it came to their appetites.

From a cultural view, Chaldean men's wives were supposed to be submissive and do exactly what their husbands requested, in bed and out of it. Bashar had a bit of old-school tradition left, but he did not mind switching roles with his wife and letting her being the dominant one at times—he loved her fire! But from day one, she'd never had a problem being submissive. When it came to anything to do with sex, the Bazzis were quite fluent in the seductive language of love.

Cyn began to stir. Opening her eyes, she smiled at seeing the state of dress she was in, but then hesitated for a moment as her thoughts raced to the wellbeing of their sons.

"I checked in on Nadia, and she's okay, but how are my babies?" she asked.

"They're fine and resting," Bashar assured her while removing the last barrier of clothing between them, leaving her completely naked.

He began to kiss his wife, while one of his hands caressed her pussy until he felt her wetness trickle down his fingers. Cyn moaned and said, "Oh God, Bashar, that feels so damn good! Please don't stop!"

"I don't plan to," Bashar whispered into her ear, then pulled back to quickly discard his pajama pants. Cyndarella grinned up at him with a devilish smile on her face. The fullness of his erection and the sight of his wife alone could cause him to climax, but what he needed now was much more than mental. He knew for sure, judging by the lustful look in her eyes, both of them needed to be fulfilled.

"Damn, I've been waiting for this since this morning. You are driving me crazy!" And she was. He had no problems letting her know it as his hands explored her body.

"Me too!" She said looking him directly in his eyes, which turned him on even more, while his fingers delved deeper into her juicy center, causing her to pant with raw desire.

Bashar began a trail of soft kisses from the top of her neck down to her hotbox, where the husky scent of his woman's pussy beckoned him. He loved her smell, and it intoxicated him even more as he licked her with precision by means of his tongue, mouth and fingers until her body trembled and she climaxed.

"Round one," Bashar said to Cyn, who managed to rebound quickly from their initial bout. Her hair had been pulled back in a ponytail, but she took off the elastic band and allowed it to fall to her shoulders because she knew how that turned Bashar on.

"Like what you see, babe? I think you're checking me out."

"Damn right. You're beautiful," he growled.

Cyndarella reached for his manhood and stroked it with her hands, telling him how big and hard he was.

"You see all of this? I want every single inch of your hardness inside me," she said. "Are you with me?" Before he could respond, Cyn pushed

Bashar back down onto the bed and reached for his member, then proceeded to consume his thick, long rod. He got off watching her as he pulled her hair back. The animalistic sounds she produced as she blew him made him want to unload, but he would hold out longer than that.

"Oh shit, I'm close," he exclaimed. He loved how skilled she was with her mouth. Cyn was so completely into orally pleasing him. Neither of them could keep their hands off each other. But he knew if she continued at the pace she was going, he would explode.

"Good," she smiled as she reached up to kiss him on the mouth. He could tell she wanted to be the dominant one tonight, but he wasn't going to allow it.

"Lie back on the bed for me, spread your legs and show me your pussy," he ordered. She complied and parted her legs, revealing a neat little patch on her freshly waxed pussy. Bashar took his cock and began teasing the entrance which was dripping with her wetness, leaving her breathless for more.

"Bazzi, now," she begged.

"Tell me what you want, babe."

"Now, I need you now. Fill me up."

Bashar eased into his wife as she wrapped her legs around his waist. Even after all the years that had gone by, her pussy's grip was like no other woman he'd ever been with. He eased his way in with slow, rhythmic thrusts, while he buried his face in her breasts and sucked on her nipples, giving each one ample attention. Cyn's vaginal walls constricted against his dick, quickening his movements.

"Please don't stop," she screamed out. He gently bit her nipples as she wrapped her muscular legs around his neck. The waves of sexual gratification heightened and rippled throughout their bodies.

"You ready to come with me?"

"Yes, Bashar, yes," Cyn moaned. "Now, please, right now!"

"No! You got to hang in there longer with me okay, Cyn? You got yours earlier, now it's my turn," he commanded.

"Fuck!" she cursed as she inclined her hips backwards a bit further to accommodate the continued hard pounding of the thickness of his meat.

Cyn couldn't keep track of how many multiples she had. Each orgasm left her weak but yearning for more. Bashar's final strokes were like the Fourth of July fireworks grand finale when he pumped a load of man juice deep within her engorged pussy, causing them both to see stars before collapsing into each other's arms and drift off to sleep.

Chapter Five

Denise sat upright with her arms folded across her chest as she listened as Dr. Shah, a fertility specialist, gave her an updated prognosis on her infertility that seemed never ending. The ongoing evaluation had extended into six long exhausting months because some of the tests had to be done within her menstrual cycle. Sean had attended most of the appointments with her and she appreciated his support, but she was relieved that he could not make the visit with her today.

Denise had been plagued with minor challenges that stood in the way of her ultimate goal of expanding her family: partial blockages in both of her tubes at one time or another, and she'd had to have her fibroids removed. Female problems were genetic in her family, and she vigorously took care of whatever ailed her when something popped up, making it a non-issue. But after she got the fibroids removed, still no luck. Health wise, everything was okay now. Dr. Shah had placed her on the fertility drug Clomid to help stimulate the ovaries by adjusting the levels of her natural hormones.

Dr. Shah had greeted her as he'd entered the room and closed the door behind him.

"Well, how am I doing, doc?"

"Clinically, you're in good health and you're ovulating regularly. Keep taking the Clomid. More than half of couples who experience this particular kind of infertility respond favorably to treatment."

"What if I am not one of those women who respond favorably? Then what? IVF is a route I don't want to take," Denise retorted.

"Denise, you're in your early forties. You are more likely to get pregnant at this time because you are taking fertility drugs. The older you are, the harder it is to conceive. Don't be concerned just yet. I can't guarantee that you will definitely conceive, but your odds are a lot better because you are here."

"Thanks, Dr. Shah. This is really important to me and my husband."

"Have lots of sex, my dear. You shall be fruitful and multiply," the physician replied in a matter of fact fashion, and ended their appointment by telling her he'd see her in a few months.

Denise had put her career ahead of family, and now she felt like she was paying the price for it. The side effects of Clomid turned her into a complete head case, with all the mood swings. She left Dr. Shah's office and went off to meet Sean for lunch to discuss this latest appointment.

Sean had become somewhat discouraged that they might not be able to get pregnant and she hated how responsible she felt for his disappointment. The waiter at Buddy's took her to the table where he was waiting. He'd ordered his favorite fried vegetables with marinara sauce, an appetizer they both loved.

"Hey, handsome," Denise offered. The two exchanged a quick kiss as she sat down.

"So we close to getting pregnant? What did the good doctor say?"

"Actually, we are a lot closer than we were. We should be pregnant within a few months."

Sean shifted in his chair for a minute, quietly in thought before he responded. "You know, Marla is twelve now. We got pregnant with her right away. I remember it like yesterday. Maybe we should just forget it."

"Sean, you can't serious! Not now! I really want to do this!" she argued.

"Denise, ain't no use in you getting upset. We have to be realistic here. Look, I wanted our kids to grow up together. Marla is twelve. That's a huge, fucking gap!" he exclaimed shaking his head.

"I know, baby, okay? Trust me, no one knows more than I do," she replied.

"You agreed, but then pulled the bait and switched routines on me as to when we'd expand our family. I'm just saying maybe we should let it go. I'm cool with that. No pressure from me."

"I was selfish. We both can attest to that. But I don't want us to give up now. At least, let's give it a couple of months to see what happens. That's all I'm asking," Denise pleaded.

"Damn right you were selfish! Look at Cyndarella and Bashar! If Bashar wanted ten kids, I know Cyn would try to give him at least half of that! You got to agree?"

"Yeah, but this is the only area in our marriage that I have been controlling. And Cyn and Bashar have different circumstances."

"Their circumstances aren't that different from ours and you know it! We all talked about wanting to have a family way back in the day. You can't have your way on this one, Dee. You need to learn that being submissive to your husband is not a bad thing. Ask Cyndarella."

She nodded her head in agreement but it stung, for as much as she admired her sister friend, she didn't like being compared to her.

Chapter Six

The couple continued their lunch with small talk, though each had their own frustration with the other. Sean resented Denise for prolonging family planning and waiting until she was forty to realize she wanted to have another baby. Now she had to rely on fertility drugs to get pregnant. Denise had put off the one thing that meant most to him, and it was a game changer for him. Fucking her now, no matter how good it was, had become an arduous task and he was debating whether he wanted any part of it anymore.

Denise sat in the parking lot at her workplace and quietly sobbed. She knew her marriage was in trouble. Sean could no longer hide his bitterness towards her anymore. That fact made her sad. In her mind, she never thought she'd ever have problems getting knocked up; thought it would be just as simple as the first time around.

Cyndarella had three kids—though technically only two if she hadn't have had the twins. Her friend didn't need fertility treatments; unlike herself, her friend was just fertile. Tavie and Vette were still single without children. Tavie didn't have kids. Vette, however, had adopted some foster children after parenting them for a year in her home.

Denise was heading up a national million- dollar ad campaign with a major soft drink company based out of California and she had to work on her presentation this afternoon. She informed her assistant to make sure she wasn't disturbed, because right now, her focus wasn't where it should be. But work was always a good elixir for her to get back on track.

The vibration of her cell phone startled her. It was Cyndarella, who was a guest speaker at an advertising symposium.

"Hey, Dee. I have a quick break, just checking in. What's going on?" she asked.

Lots going on, here with me busting my ass for you, boss lady! I'm almost finished with my soft drink presentation. It's looking good and I really think they will like it."

"Awesome! How'd your doctor's appointment go?"

"We're almost there. It's really starting to put a strain on my marriage to tell you the truth. If I don't get pregnant, Sean may not even want to stay with me!" Dee whimpered softly.

"Girl, stop! It can't be that bad! Sean wouldn't leave you if you can't get pregnant. That's bullshit!"

"It might sound like bullshit, but it's true. I waited too damn long to start trying, and now we are so not in a good space at present. I need to get back to work here. Call me later?" Denise stated, her exasperation filling her voice.

"You got it, Dee. Hang in there."

Denise missed her friends, and could use some friendship therapy right now. She was careful not to dump too much because they all had their own lives and she hated being a 'Debbie Downer' around her pals. She never was in the past, but since she'd been on Clomid, she'd been moody, somewhat depressed and now, due to the recent chain of events, scared.

Chapter Seven

The city of Detroit's bankruptcy kept Corvette busy. In fact, over the past two years, Vern Court Reporting Services, her business, had made more money than it ever had in the previous three years. Everything in her life moved without complication.

Motherhood via adoption was the route she'd chosen to take after becoming a foster mom. Lynne Reeding, the case manager assigned to her at Orleans Family Services, had asked during one of the home visits if she wanted to keep the children on a permanent basis. Though the thought hadn't really crossed her mind, the bond the children had developed with her was enough to make her say yes.

Consistency had helped transform the children and built their trust in her. It was transforming for her too. All the way down to her pockets. The state of Michigan picked up the tab for most of the occupational therapy and other special services the children needed, which was a great help.

Carly, her daughter, was twelve and Brent, eleven. They'd been nicknamed the 'crazy tweens' because they were a comedic pair. Carly, her once thin daughter was no longer the waif she'd been when Vette had originally taken her in.

The young girl had wide, big, brown eyes like Diana Ross, and a full head of black, kinky, curly hair that, for whatever reason, never grew past the nape of her neck. She'd met Carly's biological mother, Shauna, a raging alcoholic White woman who'd lost custody of four of her six children. Shauna said Carly's father was an African man from Ghana she'd met while taking classes at Washtenaw Community College, and he'd left her once Carly was born. Brent's father had died in a house fire when he was a newborn.

Brent was gangly and pale with blond hair and blue eyes. There was a shared resemblance in the kids if you looked at them hard enough. Carly had a beautiful medium complexion, but in the summer sun, like now, her daughter did not look like she was of mixed race at all! It didn't bother her as much as it seemed to bother the strangers who loved to make random comments about her parentage. They went as far as to ask what country she'd adopted them from. Even some of the mothers at the school had given Vette dirty looks because it was obvious the kids had different daddies. They accepted her into their circle when they learned she'd adopted—not that she needed their approval.

Vette's love life had stabilized in a way that she hadn't anticipated, but she wasn't complaining. Louis was her official plus one and had been for the last six and a half years. They still had separate homes, but spent a substantial amount of couple and family time together with her kids. They relied on her trusted IUDs that she'd had inserted several times throughout their relationship. She was going to change to a hormone-free IUD at her next doctor's appointment because she wanted the protection of birth control without the addition of hormones.

Louis had told Vette he didn't want to have more children since his were grown, but he'd help her out with the children. He had grandkids the same age as her kids, and she couldn't be mad at him because at least he was honest and he kept his word of being there for her, which meant quite a lot. There was this nagging part of her that appeared incomplete because she'd wanted to know as a woman what it felt like to have life move inside of her, but she resigned herself on the notion that for her, there would be no possibility of it ever happening, and she'd settled for it.

Speaking of adult children, Sonya and Harper, the two of Louis's kids she had met, were okay with her. She was white which, in 2014, unfortunately remained a big deal with them. They were mad at their

Black father for taking up with her. She hadn't met his other son because he was a Marine, deployed overseas. From what she understood from his siblings, it wasn't a must on his to-do-list, thanks to their meddling mother who slammed her every time she'd had a chance. That was a story for another day!

Baggage, everybody came with some form of it. The beauty of it was she wasn't held down by any of Lou's stuff. They had boundaries and each respected the other not to violate that line of trust. Her own mother, Tara, was not thrilled with Vette's man, or children, and often reminded her they were not hers, even though legally she'd adopted them. She'd embraced traveling down a non-traditional route, for she'd reached her goal of having a family, no matter what other people thought.

Vette grabbed the phone to call Tara to remind her about her quarterly dinner that she'd be hosting at her home next week. Tara was a nurse at Beaumont Hospital, and while at work, mostly let the phone go into voicemail which was why Vette chose to call her at the moment.

"Hello, Corvette."

"Mom, I thought you'd be working so I was going to leave you a voicemail," a rattled Vette said.

"I'm onto you, chickadee, and your little voicemail trick. I'm not stupid, you know." Her mother spoke drily.

"The Vern family dinner is next week, Saturday evening at 5:00. Don't forget!"

"You mean the friends and family dinner, don't you?"

"C'mon, mother. You are not going to do this today, you hear me? You know good and well, you always have a great time. Bye-Bye!"

Vette quickly hung up the phone. Tara was not a fan of having lots of friends around. She believed that someone was always out to get you. Her mother liked her friends, but she always seemed to be looking out of the corner of her eye to see who was throwing shade, or if she could throw shade if needed. Tara's favorite standby line to her as far as women were concerned was, "Dodge the daggers, for someone is always on the take to stab you in the back."

Vette was looking forward to seeing everyone at Tara's dinner. Tavie would be back, and based on those sexy pictures her friend had posted up on Instagram, there would be tons of stories and laughter. Albeit, as a rule, she always made sure her gal pals arrived earlier before dinner, because there were some conversations that would be reserved for their four pairs of ears only. The fellas didn't mind, especially since the Tigers game would be on, and Louis would make sure the drinks were flowing.

Chapter Eight

"**O**ctavia, move it! The car is here! Let's go!" Orville yelled out to Tavie, who quickly grabbed her handbag.

"Here I am," she offered. On the rare occasions when Orville called her by her given name, she knew he meant business. She wore a strapless turquoise mini dress, with large hoop silver earrings and a slinky silver bracelet.

"It took you long enough! Though you look beautiful, we're going to be late if we don't hurry!" her man said, before leaving their suite. Luckily, they were on the second floor and only had to walk down one story to reach the lobby where their driver for the evening was waiting for them.

The Kirkland family reunion was coming to a close tonight and they were headed off to the celebration dinner. The driver opened the door for them.

"The Ruins in Ocho Rios," Orville instructed the driver.

"Very nice choice, Mr. Kirkland. Me know some of dem Kirklands, yeah mon! Crazy bunch of good people they are," he laughed.

"True dat, true dat," Orville chimed in and joined in the laughter.

It was a forty-minute ride to the restaurant and Tavie's stomach began to growl. She hadn't eaten much today because she'd heard the food at this place was supposed to be delicious; she would over-indulge and not give a damn about it. Orville took out a joint and took a few hits of the cigar-size reefer, then put it out.

They arrived just before 6:30 at their destination, The Ruins, which was surrounded by a beautiful lush garden with over fifty species of fern plants in their very own fern gully. A tour guide showed the couple the grounds of the property, before taking them to the banquet room that the Kirklands reserved for the evening where the guests were hanging out.

"You guys ready to party?" a fifty-something well-dressed female inquired.

"Mother! You said you couldn't make it because of work!" Orville said with clear affection and excitement as he embraced the small brown-skinned woman.

"I know, but I found someone to see after my pets and I am here, darling! I couldn't resist the chance to see my only son's lady friend you speak so highly of. Octavia, correct?" she asked, extending her thin hand to Tavie.

"Hello, Dr. Kirkland. Yes, I'm Octavia Slade. It is such a pleasure to meet you," Tavie shyly greeted the woman with a quick hug.

"You can relax, young lady. You're easy on the eyes. I like what I see on the surface at least. Come, let's get better acquainted, Octavia. Orville, I want to show your lady around. See you in a bit."

Orville knew his mother held a soft place in his heart for Geneva, and though she hadn't been surprised to hear they were divorcing, was disappointed that her son and his wife couldn't make their marriage work. They'd gotten married when they were twenty—mere babies—and it had ended fifteen years later, due to their lack of commitment to each other and broken promises.

Geneva was easy to love, but complicated. She was from the neighboring town of Martha Brae in Trelawny parish. They'd met when they were youngsters. Her grandparents had lived next door to the Kirklands in Falmouth, and he'd hang out with her and brothers when they came by for a visit. The others around them saw it before they did and predicted they would be a couple, but he and Geneva always denied it, laughing it off.

That had all changed the day Orville went out to the lake to meet her brother, Harold, who to this day was still one of his best friends to go fishing with. Harold had taken ill and Geneva offered to go in his place. Geneva had on a pair of tiny denim shorts and a pink bikini top that appeared to be a size too small for her ample cleavage that peered out at him enticingly.

"Where's Harold?" Orville asked, not taking his eyes off her.

"Home. In deh bed sick." She'd spoken in their native patois.

"Why are you dressed like that?" he questioned the young girl. Surely she couldn't be trying to seduce him! Or was she? He didn't know.

"Like what?" she played along.

"Like you want me to...you know? I'm getting out of here before we both do something that we might regret." As he began to gather his things, he turned around to find Geneva was naked. It was only the second time a girl had stood in front of him nude.

"Me no virgin after today, mon. You gon be the first to have my punanny."

Geneva, even as a teenager had known how to assert herself. She wasn't about to take no for an answer, and she didn't have to. Before he could say anything, she reached for his shorts and pulled them down. That was all he allowed her to do before he took control and ended her virginity.

Chapter Nine

A shton Kirkland was a veterinarian, who'd made Miami her home. She had a thriving, high-tech hospital in a pet-friendly environment with dedicated caring professionals. A lot of high-profile, well-to-do types frequented her clinic, because in addition to wellness care she provided therapeutic alternative treatments that included massage therapy. A kennel was housed on the property, equipped with a twenty-four hour monitoring system similar to a nanny-cam system that allowed clients to check in to see how well their animals were being cared for when they were away.

She also had an organic bakery, whipping up biscuits for the dogs. Recently, Ashton had been contacted by Whole Foods to discuss a partnership for a couple of their stores in Broward County to carry her Bark Bites line of treats. The bakery made everything from sweet potato biscuits and doggy pizza to simple round bagels in a variety of flavors.

Business kept her away from her son. Though she saw him twice a year, if scheduling allowed. Ananda, her daughter, had married an Army officer within a month of meeting him a decade ago. They were currently stationed in Hawaii.

Ananda was a physical therapist at the VA hospital near Honolulu. Ashton was grateful life was good for her children. Especially Ananda, who'd recently found out she was expecting a baby. Orville worried her most. He was a good-looking, tall glass of chocolate milk, and women loved to devour him—and he loved devouring them.

Waldon, her brother, had called her and told her about the latest love in Orville's life whom, until now, she'd never met. Waldon had also confided to her that Orville was planning on marrying this woman, which bothered her a bit; it didn't appear Octavia was taking a real interest in getting to know her and she needed to know why.

"So, Octavia, please tell me how long you and my son have been together?"

"We started dating seven years ago, but we weren't exclusive right off the bat."

"I see. So when did you become exclusive, if you don't mind me asking?"

"No, I don't mind. I waited until his divorce was final, which was in 2009."

"Enough time for me to have met you by now, right? I mean, I've been to Michigan about three times since then, and O, as I prefer to call him, sees me twice a year, and why you not come with him?" she asked in her Jamaican dialect.

"Dr. Kirkland, those are valid questions. Orville has asked me to go to Miami to meet you on numerous occasions, but I admit I was nervous. I understand you still have a relationship with Geneva. I didn't want to meet you until I knew he *really* was serious about me. I am sorry if you were offended." Tavie saw the doctor's demeanor change with her declaration.

"I see you are a little sensitive about the ex-wife. I am quite fond of Geneva, and perhaps will feel the same for you in time, but that is beside the point. You feel alright now, like my son's the one?"

"Yeah, love. Am I the one?" Orville surprised the women as they talked in the atrium. "Mom, stop giving her the third degree!"

"I don't know," Tavie teased. "Are you the one?" she joked. "Of course, you're the one, silly!" And your dear mother is not giving me the third degree!"

"Well then, it's settled. I will be waiting for my wedding invitation," Dr. Kirkland replied.

"It will be soon. I gotta knock her up before she gets too old!" he joked.

"Thanks a lot! You're no spring chicken either, lad," his mother shot back. "Glad to know you plan on giving me grandchildren."

The tension faded away as they walked back into the banquet room, where Caribbean music rang out of the speakers and rum punch flowed. The illuminated soothing waterfalls combined with a plethora of food selections, including fish and chicken with Jamaican jerk as options.

The night left a lasting impression. Everything was beautifully presented. The music and drinks were nonstop. Tavie drank several drinks, but she felt like she was interviewing for a job and didn't want to get drunk in front of the Kirkland clan, even though many of them were shitfaced right now.

The dancing alone would bring anyone to their knees. Caribbean folks' dancing could captivate any crowd, and she knew had a few moves of her own that made her fit in just fine. She was also very turned on by Orville and almost had an orgasm out on the dance floor, though she managed to play it off.

Other couples looked like a pack of dogs in heat out on the floor and she had to look away. Man, was she hot right now! The dampness between her legs had soaked through her panties. She had to find a way to talk her lover into going back to the resort, A.S.A.P!

As if reading her mind, Orville came behind her and offered her another rum punch, and asked her to take a walk with him.

"Orville, I'm so horny, I can barely walk without coming! Let's leave!"

"Yeah mon! Love it when you get hot and nasty! This can't wait! C'mon wit me", Orville directed, as he took her through a winding walkway that housed an orchid deck filled with beautiful Koi fish. Behind it, out of sight, a hammock was privately located where they could do as they wished.

Orville helped Tavie onto the oversized hammock, while she hiked her dress up. His trousers fell at his knees. He stepped out of them as he climbed on top of her and guided his rock-hard dick into her womanhood. The hammock swayed with the movement of their hips, intensifying the pleasure they felt gripping their loins.

The material of the hammock scratched at her back while they fucked like wild animals. Tavie grabbed Orville's ass with her ankles in a frenzied state. He'd not seen her quite like this before. It turned him on. But he wanted to extend their rendezvous before they headed back to the party.

"I'm going to give it to you nice and slow, Tav. Just grind on my lead pipe until you can't take anymore, love."

There weren't words to describe the endless sensation her pussy was feeling. Orville's Jamaican jerk sausage was the spoon stirring her hot stew, and now the meal was about to boil over. Her trembling body thrashed back and forth in the hammock as she fought to catch her breath.

"Fuck! I'm so gone. You're turning me out!" she moaned, while Orville sucked on her brownie bite-sized erect nipples. He came a short time later and, as much as he would like to have stayed at the party, they reeked of sex. Tavie was soaking in his cum, and he could feel the succulence of her juices on his balls. He didn't want to disrespect his woman, or the kin folks. He'd cover for them, as they had to leave.

The reunion was still in full swing. The family continued living it up, dancehall style. The relatives urged them on to stay longer which they did, for an hour, then said their goodbyes. The two were tired and fell asleep on their way back to the resort. However, on their return, they managed to find their way into the shower, where they took turns washing the other. They had already packed their belongings earlier, which meant one less thing they had to do tomorrow.

They'd booked a late afternoon return flight back to Detroit so they could sleep in. Tavie didn't know what had been in the rum punch, but it was like an accelerant for her, and for the first time in her adult life, she fucked until the sun came up.

Chapter Ten

S assy, sexy dance songs played throughout Delilah's Delight Dance Studio as the ladies began to warm up. Cyndarella's guilty pleasure, which helped her maintain her weight, was the art of erotic dancing. She'd even learned a couple of sexy pole moves, though those had come after the bruises she had gotten on her thighs.

The classes had started out as something fun to do away from the kids, but soon became an outlet for her to release tensions from work and home. She had no complaints about most things. Management of personal time for she'd needed for herself had been an elusive thing. The needs of every person in her life seemed to trump those of her own and she'd gotten frustrated. The cool thing about Delilah's was the range of ages of the women, from eighteen to eighty, and their professions. Seriously! Anybody who said being sexy didn't matter hadn't lived, in her opinion.

The Bazzis had a state-of-the-art gym in their walkout basement that included a commercial grade Nordic Track elliptical machine, treadmill, adjustable bench and a set of dumbbell weights up to twelve pounds. Bashar and Cyn worked out together at least two times a week, depending on the world around them. Other times, they worked out alone, for they were both vain about their appearances.

Tonight, Itsy, the dance instructor was teaching them a new chair dance routine that was a spicy little number which met the ladies' approval.

Cyn had made a point of making everyone her friend while *in* class, but when it was over...

Some of the women wanted to go for drinks afterwards, but although decent enough, some of them were not on her level. She wasn't trying to sign up any new recruits for a mentorship on the difference between class and ass!

Cyndarella left the studio feeling energized and pumped. She hadn't told her friends about the dance classes because they already thought that she was a bonafide, freakalicious harlot, and that was fine by her! She wasn't about to continue stoking the fire any more than was needed. One thing she'd learned of late was to talk less and listen more when it came to her inner circle. She had begun applying this new concept, using a bit more restraint but not letting them feel left out.

Denise's hormones had her on edge about the least little thing. Cyn hoped that the conversation they'd had earlier about Sean was just anxiety. Sean wouldn't leave Marla and Denise, or would he? Cyn rarely stopped over anybody's house without calling, especially in a situation like this, but curiosity kept pressing at her.

Denise was sat at her computer, sipping on a latte she'd made to help ease her nerves, when she heard the doorbell prompting her to answer the caller. Peering through the peephole, she opened the door to her friend and boss.

"Is everything okay?" she asked Cyndarella.

"I don't know. You mind if I come in for a minute?"

The ladies sat down in Denise's office. Denise offered Cyn something to drink but she declined.

"I'm here. I'm worried. Not here to pry, just to let you know anything you need, come to me. We're good?"

"Sure thing. Thanks, I appreciate that. I don't want to talk about it just yet, though. Sean is on his way back with Marla. She had karate class tonight."

"Well, I'm outta of here! I came to say what I had to say. It will all work out, I really believe that. Alright, lady?"

"Dear Cyn, forever the optimist," Denise laughed. "Who would have thought being married to Bashar would bring out that side of you?" she chuckled.

"I know, right?" The two women hugged as Cyndarella left to make her way home. Cyn had the luxury of not having to spend every moment at the office, yet she did. After seeing the state Denise was in, she knew her presence was a must.

Chapter Eleven

Denise put on her suit and walked out of the bedroom without looking at Sean. She'd stayed up until 4:30 this morning working on her presentation, then sent it over to Cyn to take a look at. She was exhausted, but she'd made it up in time to see Marla had breakfast, before her daughter headed out with Kyra, the next door neighbor's kid, to their assigned bus stop at the corner for summer camp at the local YMCA.

"You not going to say good morning?" her husband asked as he walked towards his wife.

"Morning, Sean."

"Look. About yesterday, all I was trying to say is another baby might not be in God's plan for us. You are putting yourself through a lot. Hell, fibroids, blocked tubes! I support your decision to give this another go, but if you're not pregnant in two months, I need you to stop trying. It's frustrating for me too, alright?"

"I hear you. I know we were open to adoption—" Denise started before Sean interrupted her.

"Denise, I need you to hear me loud and clear. Surrogates, adoptions, you name it! All that shit is off the table, now, got it?" he lectured her. "If, say eight years ago, *someone* would have had taken our conversations about having a baby seriously, then the outcome might be different for us today," he sarcastically stated.

"You don't have to be so condescending, either, Negro!" she spat out, and then stormed away.

"I still want my goodbye kiss. Hey, come back here," Sean joked to a still-seething Denise.

"Fuck you!"

"I love you, too!" Sean giggled. They'd never had these kinds of arguments before. It posed an interesting new dynamic in their relationship.

Thing for Sean was, a promise was a promise. She'd broken hers on the very principal of their ideals and values. He couldn't force her to carry his baby, although he wished he could. The decision ultimately belonged to her. If she was willing to be this controlling, he wondered, what else would she be compelled to have power over?

They still had a little something going for them, as his dick was about to bulge out of his pants after their heated debate. Tonight, he was coming home to have his way with his wife, and she wouldn't say no. She truly was desperate to carry his seed, and he could use that to his advantage and fuck the living shit out of her ass.

Sean's thoughts were jarred by an incoming phone call. His little fantasy would have to wait until tonight, as he was running late for yet another conference call with the East Coast corporate bigwigs. He'd see if his schedule allowed him any wiggle room, for if it did, he'd talk his wife into a quickie to relieve his pent-up, yearning desire. He knew Denise wasn't happy with him right now because he had her at a disadvantage, and he was going to use it to his gain.

Chapter Twelve

Denise was delighted Cyn accepted the final presentation for the soft drink account; so much so, she insisted that Dee take the day off. Denise complied, and went out to get a manicure and pedicure at the local Korean nail salon in town. Sean had really gone too far this time, she thought to herself. Pampering helped, but didn't lift her spirits much or take her mind off it.

Natalie sent her a quick message that Sean'd had a floral arrangement delivered. Denise told her assistant to keep them. Flowers wouldn't make her feel better, but the least she could do was to acknowledge them.

"Hello," he answered.

"Thanks for the flowers."

"So you still mad?"

"Hell, yeah! What the fuck do you think?"

"Calm down, woman! You're so mean, but it's actually turning me on!" he chuckled. "Where you at?"

"You're so nasty! I'm not telling you where I'm at!"

"I'll find your Black ass, you can believe that. See you later, and I'll make you play nice."

He had some nerve to start in on her and now he expected her to give it up! As mad as she was, she started to get aroused, which in her case was a good thing. She needed all the loving she could get, but would it produce the baby she so yearned for?

Denise went out for a run, which wasn't that good for her worn-out knees. She could only run about a mile now because they bothered her. She had lost a couple of dress sizes and was down to a ten. If she maintained between a size ten and twelve, she knew she'd look fine.

It was almost noon which meant a quick nap before Marla got home. They would have takeout for dinner tonight because she did not feel like cooking.

Sean had called Natalie, who'd confirmed that his wife wasn't in the office today as he suspected. He'd been working long hours as the National Sales Manager for three radio stations. Having an android and iPad made his days productive during the time he spent travelling. But when he was in town, he took advantage of going in to the office to keep his finger on the pulse. This afternoon, even though it was unplanned, he would be working from home—and it wasn't the usual kind of work that was on his agenda.

The garage door opened and he saw Dee's Audi QX6 was parked.

"A good sign, my brother," Sean said aloud to himself. He removed his clothes downstairs in the guest bathroom off the living room and marched upstairs. Denise didn't like anything more than a sheet on her since she'd started on Clomid, and he pulled the sheet back to expose her reddish-brown, voluptuous body beneath it.

Numerous freckles splattered on her body, though they weren't as pronounced as in the later summer months when she stayed out in the sun, which darkened them, to her delight. The freckles were beautiful to him and looked like fragmented pieces of the sun had kissed her body. The roundness of her ass appeared like moons that faced him as she slept. Kneeling down, Sean began to place soft kisses on her butt cheeks. His tongue traced the outer edges as he slowly nibbled at them, causing her to awaken.

"Oh, shit! You startled me. I didn't know you were here! Horny bastard! I really didn't take you that serious!"

"I was. I am. Turnover on your stomach." She did as she was told, as Sean's tongue began to trace around her neck and down her spine, sending chills throughout her body. He began to massage her thighs, methodically making a path to her vagina which was so wet that he could see the sap glistening on her pussy lips.

"Lay on your back for me," he asked. Once again he placed a trail of kisses with his mouth and tongue down her body until he reached her cunt. He rubbed his nose in it, for he loved the musky, aromatic smell coming from it. He began to lick her ever so softly and gently, while finger-fucking her. Denise writhed in bliss in front of him. Then she sat up and looked him and went right at his 'trick stick', the nickname she gave his junk, 'cause he could do anything with his stick to make her come.

Denise took the wide mushroomed tip of his penis deep within her mouth and began sucking him as if her mouth were a substitute for her hole. Sean almost came, though like a pro she sensed it and pulled back for a moment, but went at it again, long enough to extract some pre-cum that she lapped away at as she stared up at him.

"Cocky little bitch, aren't you?"

"That's what you love about me, don't you?" she retorted. In response, Sean grabbed her by the waist, drawing her in with her rear facing him.

"I'm about to break your fucking back!" he bellowed out.

"Bring it on, motherfucker! Bring it on, then!"

"Oh, you bad now, huh?"

"Bring it on!" she shouted again.

"I'm gonna fuck the dog shit out of you, talking shit to me like that."

"Ah! Ah! Ah! Ah!" she gasped, barely able to catch a breath

"That's all you got to say now, huh?" he hollered.

"I going to come!" she tossed back to him, curving her backside further on his trick stick. Repositioning herself, she slowly propped up her ass and arched her back with movements that simulated an ocean wave current in the direction that she flowed. Like a volcano erupting with lava, Sean gushed all of his sperm within the confines of her vaginal cavity.

They continued to share an intimate afternoon together before they went off to pick Marla up from day camp. Neither of the mentioned anything pregnancy related, they just chilled. Sean believed their afternoon tryst reconfirmed the desire they had for each other. He loved his wife, and when she went hard at him, as she had this afternoon, there wasn't a woman around that could fuck like her!

Chapter Thirteen

T he caterers stopped by to set up the food for the evening. Vette had planned on cooking, but her caseload was tremendous, and if her heart wasn't in it, she felt like it would affect the outcome of the food. She knew her loved ones wouldn't have a problem with a potluck, but she did. Louis had planned on grilling some goodies, but it had rained all week.

Vette still marveled at her new home, which she'd purchased five years ago in Bloomfield Township. She used to live in Royal Oak and had tried to find something there within her price range, but she couldn't find a thing and she didn't want to rent. She placed offers on homes in neighboring Troy and Berkley and she was outbid on too many to count! There was one in particular she'd had her heart set on, but it was a short sell which dragged on longer than she could stand, forcing her to withdraw her offer.

The charming ranch she'd eventually purchased had a large backyard with three bedrooms and two and a half bathrooms. It was also right off of Square Lake and Woodward, which was a straight shot to the Oakland and Wayne County courts. If she had to go to Wayne County in Detroit, to avoid I-75, all she had to do is hop on Woodward for thirty minutes or so, and she was there.

The ranch was only one thousand, seven hundred square feet, but it had a finished basement and a Florida room that made the home feel more spacious than it was. Besides that, they lived in the Bloomfield Hills school district, one of the best in the state. There were excellent resources for her kids and she was committed to keeping them in a safe and stimulating learning environment.

Vette selected a favorite staple in her closet to wear: an asymmetric Madison Marcus color- blocked pink and orange maxi dress that featured a peek-a-boo hem, showing off a little bit of her tanned legs. She wore her shoulder-length highlighted blond hair down, and chose the two-carat diamond earrings that Louis had given her, along with a gold chunky bracelet. She didn't know which bottle of perfume she grabbed but she sprayed a blast of something on her neck, and headed down to the games room to check on the children who were playing there.

The layout of the home included an open floor plan with a generous eat-in kitchen, in lieu of a formal dinner room. The kitchen was big enough for a table of eight and had counter space to seat an additional four on bar stools. Louis had provided financial relief to her by matching the $25,000 payment she'd used as a down payment. The combination of funds equaled $50,000. That made a huge dent in her monthly mortgage, and for a residence in Bloomfield Township, she only paid $120 more per month than for her previous bungalow in Royal Oak.

The décor came courtesy of IKEA. They had some really neat furnishings that didn't break the bank. She took her friends with her to the showroom in Canton, but Cyndarella said she wouldn't be caught in there! But she decorated the home so well that even Cyndarella was surprised most of her buys were furnished by IKEA.

Vette did miss walking in family-friendly downtown Royal Oak. That diverse area offered numerous restaurants, a movie theater, zoo and cultural events. However, she did not miss the congestion. Parking was limited, and in the summer it started to get a little crazy for her liking. The kids enjoyed going back to see their old friends or visit some of their former haunts. They still went back to Holiday Market to pick up some goods from the bakery. The new area had been an adjustment for the kids, as would be expected, but the neighborhood children had welcomed them right into the fold in the subdivision.

The biggest question she dealt with was that damned M-word, as in *marriage*. Louis knew it, and so did every other person around them. It didn't matter whether it was someone in the schools or at work, wherever or whenever the question could be asked, it was. She had no answers. The only thing that did make her feel a tad bit better about it was the fact that she wasn't alone; Tavie was under the spotlight too! Orville had best make it soon for Tavie, or she would walk. And for her, it was only a matter of time, she hoped. She wasn't a fucking male mind reader, and she wasn't the type of woman who believed in giving Louis an ultimatum. She'd simply find a husband elsewhere and it would be on him if he lost out!

Chapter Fourteen

T he guests gathered at the Verns' home for dinner, and sat in the living room as each arrived. Smooth jazz permeated throughout the house. Louis and Vette had beer, wine and margaritas on hand for the thirsty adults. Vette made a pitcher of lemonade with freshly squeezed lemons for the kids to enjoy.

She'd ordered a spread of Mexican food from Mexican Fiesta, an award winning authentic restaurant in Pontiac. She got the kids a taco bar because most of the ones who were in attendance were picky eaters.

"Man, Tavie, look at that tan, girl! You're so dark and lovely!" Vette laughed.

"I did get a little color on me, y'all. But I look good, right?"

"Hell, yeah!" Denise chimed in.

"We're just a group of good looking motherfuckers," Bashar said.

"Vette. I love that dress! You look great!" Cyn piped in.

"But she still has a flat ass and that dress might hide it, but it won't change it!" Tara wise-cracked.

"There, there now, Ms. Tara. I like what she's working with. She's alright by me," Louis supported his woman.

Checking out Cyndarella, Vette couldn't help notice she appeared a size smaller, as she observed her friend's designer black cutout maxi dress that she looked stunning in. Marla and Carly had gotten to be fast friends, and big sisters to Nadia. Mrs. Bazzi senior was babysitting the twins tonight.

Louis's colleague, Scott, a partner in his law firm, was also in attendance and appeared to be taken with her mother. Tara gave the impression she was pleased with the attention the mature African American gentleman was giving her.

As the guests sat down for supper at the table, the children made a beeline for the kitchen.

"Mom, we want to watch Catching Fire on Netflix. Can we?" Carly asked.

"Can we, Mom?" Brent joined in.

Vette asked Cyndarella and Bashar if it would be alright for Nadia to watch the mildly violent movie, and they agreed. Louis poured more margaritas as they ate dinner, while endless chatter filled the room.

"So, how was Jamaica, Tavie?" Sean asked.

"Beautiful! It was so relaxing. We had the best time ever! It really was unforgettable."

"Yeah mon. It was all irie," Orville replied.

"I hated it when I was there! Do the people still beg you on the island for money? It was pretty scary for me when I went a few years ago," Tara said.

"That's really de flavor of Jamaica, or any place you go in the Caribbean. No disrespect to tourists. That's their hustle," Orville explained.

Orville and Tavie shared pictures of their vacation. It was apparent this trip had brought them closer. Orville had been around for a minute now, but no one knew what was next for either Tavie or herself with their dates. The men got up to watch the Tigers game, and the ladies gathered around to finish their chat from earlier in the afternoon. Vette hoped her mother wouldn't feel the need to flap off at the mouth during their girl talk.

"So Denise, are you knocked up yet?" Vette questioned.

"Would I be drinking margaritas if I were?"

"Oops! Sorry! I know you've been trying," Vette apologized.

"And trying, and trying. But hey, that's the fun part!" Dee groaned.

"Cyn, those babies must be wearing you out! You're looking awfully thin since the last time I saw you," Tara offered.

"Uh, yes, Tara, the kids are keeping my metabolism up, but I am not much thinner. I'm still a size eight," Cyn explained.

"She works out just about every other day as well," Denise added.

"Well, I've watched you all grow into amazing strong women. I'm really proud of you! You've done well, girls. All I ask is that you keep it up. Whatever you're doing, it's working," Tara suggested.

The women appreciated hearing the heartfelt admiration from Tara, a hellcat who said it like she meant it.

"Tavie, it's really good seeing how connected you are with Orville. You guys have come a long ways," Cyn validated.

"I'm just glad to see you finally left that asshole, Mack!" Denise spat.

"Me too! Try telling that to my mother, though. She told me she did not trust me dating any foreigners because they are sneaky liars. She is not a fan of my relationship. She will tell anyone who'll listen, Africans and Jamaicans are shifty and known for screwing every stupid woman that they come in contact with." It hadn't helped that she'd told her mother about Geneva, the hussy who was an indirect catalyst in helping end her relationship with Mack.

"What about you, Corvette? You and Lou look pretty cozy. If he has it this good, where is his incentive to be in it for the long haul?" her mother asked.

"Mom. He's here, isn't he?" Vette quipped rather flippantly to her mother, who was on a roll. "I can't ask for more than that. Lou is with me all the time. If he wasn't, now that would be a problem."

"Well, if you ask me, I say that both Louis and Orville have test driven the cars long enough for you and Tavie. You know what I mean? What the hell are they waiting on? Maybe you should take away the key from the ignition is all I am saying."

Shifting uncomfortably in her seat, Tavie felt compelled to address Tara in a firm but respectful way.

"Tara, believe it or not, I agree with you. However, tonight, we are here to have a good time and not dwell on our marital statuses, if you don't mind. It's kind of personal."

"You mean painful, don't you? Understood. It is personal, but we all see the same thing. Nothing! I'm sure I can speak on behalf of your parents, Tavie, in saying that we do want to be alive when our daughters decide to get married. I know I do," Tara countered, raising her voice loud enough so that the men in the other room could hear them. With that, Tara excused herself to see her grandkids. Afterwards, she bid farewell to the group and headed out for the evening, but not before exchanging phone numbers with Scott.

As they chattered amongst themselves, Vette couldn't help notice Cyndarella wasn't as talkative as the others had been. As if reading her mind, her friend begin to speak.

"I hate to admit it, but your mom was right, Vette. I really want the best for you and Tavie. Are you guys even talking about your future?" Cyndarella inquired.

"Once in a while we do. I trust Lou to keep his word about moving forward at some point," Vette answered. "I can't force him. It's his decision to make when he feels like he's ready."

"So when are you going to make him accountable about a reasonable timeframe, Vette? And what about you, Tavie?" Denise questioned. "This is starting to get old!"

"We know, so let's just drop it tonight," Vette sighed.

"It isn't any of our business, so I'm fine staying out of it. Just remember, men can only get away with what you allow them to. It's not entirely on them," Cyndarella reckoned.

"I'll toast to that!" Tavie said, holding up her margarita glass, toasting with her friends in solidarity. "But all joking aside, I look forward to the craziness that comes with being a bride, and having a wedding that people will talk about for time to come, like you had, Cyn. I just have to be patient just a teeny bit longer."

"Here's the thing you have to remember." Cyndarella spoke in a solemn tone. "Be careful of who you're saying 'I do' to. The commitment is between you and whoever you marry *and* all the demons and baggage both of you drag in with you. The ceremony and wedding gown aren't even a dress rehearsal for what married life truly represents or is even about."

The ladies were captivated by the seriousness of their friend and drew nearer to listen to what she was saying.

"Once the well-wishers disperse and that designer tuxedo and expensive gown come off, all that is left is husband and wife. That is where the real commitment begins between the two of you, and compromise and flexibility become your new best friends. Don't let the pageantry of a wedding cloud your judgment of the facts."

"She's so right," Dee said. "That's why so many marriages end up in divorce."

"Cyn, you scared the hell out of me, but I needed to hear it."

"Me too," Tavie agreed.

THE MEN MADE A RUCKUS in the family room, where they were watching the Tigers game. They could be heard making bets on the Tigers winning the World Series.

"As long as Miggy stays healthy, how can we lose?" Louis asked.

"That man is playing the best in Major League Baseball right now." Sean spoke. "Don't get any better than Miggy. But they got to stay healthy, and Prince Fielder's got to stop doing dumb shit."

"We got to check out a playoff game. I can get us some tickets. Let me know if you're in," Bashar told them.

The men agreed in unison that they would go to a game and have their ladies join them downtown for dinner and drinks. Whenever they had a chance to make a fun day out of it, they remembered to include the women, and they often joked about how well they would be rewarded later when they each went home.

Chapter Fifteen

"I heard what Tara said last night about marriage. I tell you, she is really something," Orville said to Tavie.

"She is, but you have been driving my ride around the block here for a minute."

"Let's just go ahead and get married. I ain't wit dat long engagement crap. Just marry me," he proposed.

"I would like a *ring,* for crying out loud! And I don't mind something simple." The telephone interrupted their conversation, and Orville told Tavie to answer as he left the room. It was her mother on the phone, and Tavie told her she needed to call her back.

"Company again, huh? It's that damn Jamaican, right?" Her mother made it clear she did not trust Orville. Nor did she trust any man with an accent, for that matter, to date her only child.

"Mom!"

"Mom, my ass! All those dreadlocks on his head, Octavia, I don't see how you could do it! Girl, they look so nasty! You better watch that sneaky motherfucker! Call me later. Bye!" Her mother hastily ended the call.

Tavie placed the cordless phone back on its cradle. When she turned around, Orville was standing on one knee in front of her asking for her hand and presenting her with a one-carat diamond solitaire, nestled in a black velour ring box.

"Octavia Slade, will you marry me?"

"Hell, yes, Orville Kirkland! I will marry you!" Tavie shouted, as joy washed throughout her body. She always wondered how she'd feel once he proposed, other than relieved, but this was nothing like it.

"So, you want to call your mother back and let her know?"

"Did *you* let my parents know you were going to do this?"

"No. Guess I should have, but we can drive up and take them to dinner and tell them together."

Tavie's father liked Orville, and he'd be cool with the marriage, but her mother, not so much. She was glad he'd answered the phone and accepted the dinner invitation for tomorrow on such short notice. It wouldn't be a good thing to prolong sharing their good news. They'd drive up and tell it.

"I got the ring in Jamaica. My mother approved of it and thought you'd love it!"

"Gosh! I kind of got the feeling you were going to propose at The Ruins restaurant back in Ocho Rios. It was so beautiful and all."

"Actually, I was. But you were such the temptress, all I could think of was hitting the skins".

The ring fit Tavie perfectly. She took a picture of it and sent texts to all of her friends t0 say that she was getting married. She'd hold off posting pictures up on Instagram until after they'd spoken with her family. The evening continued with the celebratory couple making a phone call to Orville's mother, who wished them well. They shared a bottle of Cristal champagne, followed by emotional, yet sexy and intimate play, which they enjoyed on and off throughout the night.

The next afternoon, they enjoyed the drive to Okemos, off I-96, was quite sunny and pleasant. The hour and a half journey took about fifteen minutes longer than it normally did because of the construction narrowing the four-lane highway down to two.

Tavie's mind wandered during the drive on the highway to her friends. The ladies had been hyped about the engagement, including Vette, whom Tavie knew had to feel jealous. They were the last two of the bunch to wed, and they had held each other up by venting. And now Vette was the last single one standing.

Orville affectionately rubbed her leg occasionally as it seemed to break the tension of the moment. She took off her ring, as she knew both her parents would spot it. They probably suspected it; anyway, as it was rare that Tavie would drop in on them on such little notice with her man in tow. There was not a cloud in the sky, which she hoped meant a good omen for them, she thought, as they pulled up at the Slades' home.

Orville opened the trunk of the black Lincoln SUV and reached inside to bring out souvenirs from Jamaica to take to his soon-to-be in-laws. Mrs. Slade was already looking out of the front screen door as they made their way to the door.

"Hey, Mom!" Tavie said, as she managed to get a hug from her uptight, rigid mother.

"Hello, Mrs. Slade. Nice to see you," Orville greeted.

"Hello Orville. Tavie. Your father's out in the backyard. He decided to grill since it's such a nice day today. Why don't we go and join him?"

They made their way to the spacious backyard that led onto a two-story deck where Mr. Slade had chicken breasts and salmon on the grill, next to the patio dining table and chair set. As they sat down, Tavie handed her parents the souvenirs from Jamaica, including spiced rum, rum cream and Blue Mountain coffee.

"Y'all, this is real nice. Should I open this now and get drunk while you are here, or wait until you leave?" Mr. Slade tried to break up the rigidity with a jovial icebreaker. "All kidding aside, thanks for thinking of us. What brings you two here?" he asked.

Mr. Slade had an intimidating presence. At sixty-five, he maintained a youthful appearance, and if it weren't for the few strands of gray throughout his hair, he could pass for being ten years younger. Tavie had told him that before, and he went to a barber who dyed his hair. Her mother was not pleased, as her father, already a chick magnet, received even more attention.

"Either you're pregnant or getting married. Correct?" Mrs. Slade said.

"The latter is correct. Mr. and Mrs. Slade, your daughter, Octavia, and I would very much like your consent to marry," Orville replied.

"That depends on what Octavia wants," her mother said, unimpressed.

"I said yes!"

"Congratulations are in order then," Mr. Slade said. "But make sure you take good care of our baby girl. Keep her happy, and you'll have a good life. Do I make myself clear?"

"But of course. We will work hard to have a happy marriage, with longevity, just like yours."

"Are you still living up in Saginaw?" Mrs. Slade inquired.

"My job transferred me to Port Huron more than a year ago. I live right by the Blue Water Bridge. I cover the whole thumb area of the state, as well as Southeastern Michigan.

"Orville, I don't want to judge you by all I hear about island men, but honestly, I do. Let me be frank, it's going to take some time before I will be truly comfortable with the whole marriage thing. But our daughter said yes, and though it may take some time, I'll get there."

The family placed their issues aside and enjoyed a delicious dinner and evening together, before heading back to Auburn Hills. As they exchanged hugs, Mrs. Slade whispered a warning in her daughter's ear.

"Keep your eyes open and don't be a fool for this dude! Make sure you have your sneakers on standby too, so when Orville fucks up—and I know his kind, he will—run like hell!"

Tavie shook her head and avoided further eye contact with her mother as Orville opened the car door for her. The drive home was easier, as there was less construction as they headed back east on the highway. Orville noticed Tavie had seemed down since they'd left her parents' home, but he assured her that everything would be irie for them. She had no doubts about Orville, for she knew lots about him, including the good, bad and ugly, and that awareness made her feel safe and secure. It was those moments with her mother that made her cast doubt on herself and the man in her life. Though Tavie swore silently to herself, she wasn't having it. If her mother couldn't respect the life she had chosen with Orville, she might just lose her daughter

Chapter Sixteen

The ladies agreed to meet that evening at Fleming's Restaurant to celebrate Tavie's engagement. Cyndarella chose a central location in Birmingham. She'd worked from home today so that she would be able to have more time to spend with the children once she completed her numerous tasks.

There were never enough hours in a day because the kids could not get enough mommy time, leaving her feeling guilty and exhausted for being so driven. This weekend was going to be all about family, as the Bazzis were invited to her parents' home to attend their annual garden party, and her brother, Pete, was here for a visit from Minneapolis.

Cyndarella thought back to last Saturday and about the comments that had been made about her weight. She didn't like it. She worked out and tried to eat right. The babies had put weight on her. The first pregnancy with Nadia had presented her with forty pounds of extra weight. The twins had doubled that, and it had taken her almost a year to get it all off. But she remained determined.

Eating was such a personal thing for her. She didn't like people looking over her shoulder to see what she was eating, or how much. This evening she decided to dress in something that wouldn't be form-fitting. She put an INC outfit together that she had gotten from Macy's. The geometric bold print wide-leg pants were soft and seductively adorned her body. The casual V-neck black tee shirt was ruched at the side seams, giving her a stylish and comfortable look.

Bashar had taken the children out to Orchard Lake to his brother's lakefront home so the children could play with the rest of their cousins. It seemed everybody was a cousin to the Bazzis. Cyndarella had learned to speak a bit of Arabic because she wanted her children to learn the language. It was a part of their tradition, who they were.

They were an interracial family, blending two cultures together, and it had its moments in the eyes of today's society. There were some days where she'd get the dirtiest looks from either Black or White people. They'd look at them with such hate, and she truly felt sorry for them because they did not know who she was, and she was not the type to give anybody a rundown. She just knew if it went beyond a dirty look, either she or her husband would have to protect their family if it came down to it.

The United States had finally elected its first Black president, Barack Obama. But interestingly enough, he was catching it on both sides. Some Blacks felt he wasn't doing enough to address issues facing their world. And their White counterparts in Congress obstructed and scrutinized every decision that he made, making it one of the worst Congresses ever in American history. Ignorance was just as deadly as a fatal disease and it was one of the reasons, Cyn was convinced, that had birthed and fed generational racism throughout the years. She wouldn't trade her family life for anything in the world!

"Over here, Cyn," Denise called out, waving her hand and motioning her over to the table.

Cyndarella sat at the table with all the women.

"Let me see your ring!" Cyn insisted, after sharing a quick hug with Tavie.

"Check this bling out, ladies! My man did good!" Tavie threw up her hand, exposing the sparkler. "I wanted to wait till we were all here to tell you how he did it. He had the ring when we were on vacation, but it wasn't the right time. Then he heard that comment Tara made, and he informally asked me to marry him."

"Tara was on a roll about everything. That's my mother. But at least something came out of it for one of us," Vette reasoned sarcastically.

"You and Louis have solidified your relationship. An engagement can't be far off for you two," Denise suggested. Vette was not her animated self, yet she kept a humorous attitude. As the ladies' drinks arrived, they ordered appetizers.

"Let's toast Tavie!" Vette requested, and they raised their glasses in agreement. Their blond friend continued, "Don't feel sorry for me. Feel sorry for him because I am not going to hang around forever. He is fifty-two!"

"Old enough to know what the fuck he wants to do," Denise threw out. "But I have to give the man the benefit of the doubt. I really think he is planning on asking you."

"So, what kind of wedding are you going for?" Cyndarella asked.

"Simple, laid-back, but elegant," Tavie shared. "We want to do it within the next three months."

"So what do you need from us?" Cyndarella asked, for she hated people requesting last minute shit from her.

"Just continue to be there for us. Oh, and a kick-ass shower! But seriously, I doubt Orville and I will have a traditional wedding. We don't want any attendants standing up for us, just our closest family and friends."

"Oooh, I am so relieved!" Cyn exclaimed. "I sure as hell don't want to be a forty-something-year-old bridesmaid!"

"I'll cosign on that shit!" Dee added.

"Well, when Louis or whoever proposes to me, and if we all happen to be in our fifties, I know one damn thing, every single one of you bitches will be my bridesmaids, ugly dresses, and all!" Vette affirmed.

"Done!" Cyndarella shouted as the women roared with laughter.

The entrees and drinks came out, as the ladies continued their night together.

"I really needed this tonight," Denise spoke out. "Sean and I decided we are going to stop trying for a baby in a couple of months if I don't get pregnant."

"Wow, are you okay with that?" Vette queried.

"We both are. That Clomid ain't no joke, shit! What about you Tavie? You think you and Orville will start trying right away?"

"Yep. It's late in the game for us, so we'll be fine with one, unless I end up pregnant with twins, like Ms. Cyndarella and her handsome fella!" Tavie hollered out as the friends laughed.

"Oh, you are *real* funny. Bashar and I were just as surprised as everyone else. Twins run in our families though and I didn't take any fertility drugs," Cyn retorted.

"Fertile bitch!" Denise mocked.

"Just rub it in, why don't you!" Dee mocked.

"And it is for that very reason, I use birth control, and next year I am getting my tubes tied!"

"Oh, I don't know Cyn," Vette teased. "I bet you $100 that you get pregnant within the year." All the women chimed in backing her, getting in on the bet.

"There is no fucking way! That is one bet you will *lose*, so get ready to pay out my loot!" Cyn countered, while making note of the date in her iPhone. "Trust me, this time next year, I'm tracking each one of you smartasses down!"

Chapter Seventeen

"**O**ctavia, you look good in just about every gown you've tried on," Mrs. Slade said to Tavie, as she modeled wedding gowns for her mother.

"It's so hard to choose just one!" Tavie exclaimed with exasperation.

"Are you talking about men, or these wedding gowns?" her mother joked.

"Mom! You know I'm talking about the gowns!"

"And it's a damn shame!" Mrs. Slade continued, but stopped her foolery when she noticed her daughter tense up. "So, when's the big day, Octavia?"

"Honestly, we're still deciding. But one thing for sure, we don't want you and Daddy paying for anything. All we want is for you to show up."

"That's commendable, but your father and I have been saving up for this, and I can assure you that we will be helping you pay for the wedding. I was surprise but honored you actually asked me to be here with you to try on gowns, and not your friends."

"Aw, Mom! This is our moment. The girls will love what I wear, no matter what. It's you being here with me that means more than anything."

"You're making me proud, girl," Mrs. Slade offered to her daughter, water filling to the brims of her eyes.

Mother and daughter spent the day together looking at wedding gowns, and discussing wedding venues, before Tavie left and headed back down home. The dress was at least out of the way now as she'd purchased a designer sample right off the showroom. Orville had wanted to go back to Jamaica to The Ruins and exchange nuptials, but due to time constraints, they decided to opt for someplace closer to home.

Tavie sat on her favorite gray Lazy Boy sofa with yellow cushions and began checking off the bridal checklist she had in her wedding planner. Orville had begun packing his belongings at home, but was planning on coming down from Port Huron later on this evening or in the morning.

She'd kept her pastor up-to-date on her marital status and he was happy for them. The ironic part of it was that her pastor was also a childhood friend. Junior was the son of the Slades' former family pastor, Reverend Edwin Bradley, Sr., when they'd lived in Southfield.

The Slade family had attended Southfield Baptist Church until Tavie graduated from high school and her parents moved up to Okemos. The Bradleys and Slades spent a lot of time together when she was a kid. Tavie could still remember sleepovers with Katie Bradley and Junior. They'd had the best of times, and now Junior was going to marry her to Orville.

Senior Bradley had passed away more than twenty years ago. She thought her mother had taken the news pretty hard, as he used to be her boyfriend back in the day. But he'd chosen Paula, an unattractive but kind-hearted woman over her mother, breaking her heart after Paula had gotten pregnant. Rumor had it, Paula Bradley had pretended to befriend Tavie's mother to get next to Senior Bradley, her then boyfriend, while they were in high school. It was a running joke that her own dear father was sloppy seconds and that the Slade marriage wouldn't last, but they'd proved everyone wrong.

Her mother forgave the pastor, and remained friends with him and his wife. If it were Tavie, she couldn't have remained friends with Pastor Bradley, let alone attend his church. Pastor Bradley was easy on the eyes, but then her dad was too! She remembered her junior high, and teachers blushing in his presence. The female teachers totally ignored her mother, which really hadn't bothered Mrs. Slade, as long as it translated into an A+ grade for Tavie. Orville and Tavie had spoken to Junior and he'd agreed to let them use the church if they wanted to marry there, or any other locale they'd select.

Tavie was so immersed in wedding stuff that she almost didn't hear the faint sound of the doorbell. She lived in a gated community and she wasn't expecting any guests other than Orville, who already had a key. Whoever it was would not go away.

It was rare that a visitor would get through the gate without Security calling, so she wondered if it was Cyndarella, who'd sold her the bachelorette pad. The person ringing the bell was relentless, which pissed her off even further as she made her way to the door. The revelation of the persistent guest made her stomach sank when she saw who the uninvited visitor was.

"Hello, Tavie. Long time, no see, eh?" Geneva drawled in her Caribbean-accented voice.

"What are you doing here? How'd you get through security?" Tavie questioned. Geneva brushed past Tavie and came into her home.

"We need to talk. First, let me say congratulations, as I hear you are getting married to my ex-husband."

"Geneva, my engagement to your ex-husband still doesn't tell me what the fuck you're doing here! How'd you even find out where I lived?" Tavie asked, while giving the woman a once over. For as much as she hated the bitch, the woman still looked very well. The trademark braids were replaced by a sleek hairstyle, with a center part which extended down beyond her shoulders.

"Well, I can see you haven't changed a bit. Uncle Waldon had you pegged one hundred per cent. You are one rigid and uptight twit," Geneva declared, angering her host.

"I don't believe he said that!"

"Let's skip the pleasantries, dearie, shall we? Orville is the father of my son. That is why *I* am here. He doesn't know it yet, but I shall tell him the truth. It's 'bout time you knew about it, too. I mean, you will be a stepmother to our son."

"Bitch, you are outta your Goddamn mind! Orville is not the father of your child! You were divorced when you got pregnant, and you had a boyfriend on top of that!"

"Speaking of on top of, I wasn't divorced when my husband and I did the nasty and made our little one. Lemme tell you, the week before our divorce, we spent every night together," Geneva buzzed.

"You're a jealous, vicious liar, Geneva, and it's pretty pathetic. I feel sorry for you, but you need to leave before I kick your ass!"

"I'll leave in due time, but there are things you need to know. I'll tell you. Believe it or not, this isn't easy for me, you know." Taking a deep breath, Geneva sighed before continuing, "Well, I must say you might want to think again before accusing me of lying. Remember how you kept calling Orville and leaving messages on his home voicemail to see if he was okay because you were so *worried* about him? You shouldn't have been. I was making sure I was doing my wifely duties! Heh, heh, heh," Geneva laughed at Tavie, who looked like she was about to vomit.

"Why tell me now? Why didn't you say something sooner to Orville if he has a son?" a winded Tavie sputtered out.

"Because Orville has decided on making you relevant, that's why! Even though our divorce was final in 2009, we still, well, you know, up until 2012, when he moved from Saginaw to Port Huron when he got transferred." The animated woman looked at Tavie with a bit of regret momentarily as she collected her thoughts. "Orville had dinner with us at least once a week for years. I made his favorite meals. Curry chicken with peas and rice. Though he never asked, I believe he knows he's Nathan's father."

"What were you? Dessert? You're one of the most hateful, miserable women I've ever met in my life! Please leave!"

"Gladly! I will leave, but Mack didn't find me so miserable, neither did Orville. And by the way, our child will know he was conceived while we were married," Geneva said, as she pulled out her child's birth certificate which listed Orville Kirkland as the child's father.

"Like it or not, I am *always* going to be a part of Orville's life, through our child, and well, I'll spare you the rest", Geneva vowed, as she walked out the door, leaving Tavie crushed.

Tavie's head began to spin and her knees felt as if they were buckling under her, as she sat down on her sofa. Orville never stopped screwing Geneva half the time he was with her! Why did he even bother divorcing her? Tavie wondered to herself.

Feelings of contempt rose within her as she thought back to the weeks leading up to his divorce. Orville had told her that he needed space to reflect on the dissolution of his marriage. She called to check up on him but he didn't return her calls as often. However he updated her via text message to pacify her that he was okay and would be in touch with her soon. This was the first red flag that had alarmed her, for he'd always found time to speak to her on the phone at least once a day. But that week had been the exception to the rule and now she understood why.

Just like her mother warned, Tavie had been played by another cheating, lying man claiming he'd loved her. There was no way she could marry Orville. She didn't want to even see him. She sent him a text and asked him to call his ex-wife, and to give her space. The locksmith would be there soon to change the locks and she'd make sure security did not let him into the complex. Ever!

Tavie closed her eyes as tightly as she could while she digested the horror of what had just transpired in her home. The serene environment was tranquil no more as the realization drove her into a fit of rage when, by chance, she casually glanced at framed pictures of herself and Orville as a couple. She began destroying everything in her presence by breaking the frames and ripping up any pictures in her sight. Once again, she'd fallen victim to a man's foolery, and as much as she longed to be in the right relationship, she felt it no longer necessary to bother trying in light of her ill-fated circumstance.

Chapter Eighteen

Cyndarella and Wiyad were on their way to meet both her husband, and brother-in-law, Faisal, in downtown Plymouth to look at an old hotel that was up for auction. It was a smaller boutique type that needed lots of work, but Bashar thought it could be a place they could renovate and turn into a money maker. The sixty-five-bed hotel also had office space that currently was being rented out.

The women lost count of time as they ate lunch at a nearby bistro and rushed out once they realized they were going to be late. Wiyad and Cyndarella were BFFs again, and that made the ladies very joyful. Wiyad had been the catalyst who'd brought Bashar back in Cyn's life, and they were both grateful to his cousin for reuniting them.

Downtown Plymouth was small and quaint. People flocked there for the ice festival in the winter, and it was a great place to grab a good meal with family, or a drink with friends. The hotel was located by the train tracks, and the noise annoyed Cyndarella as they found a parking spot in the back of the lot.

Cyndarella grabbed her Tom Ford black round-rimmed sunglasses and put them on, before shutting the door of her Range Rover. Wiyad told her how she approved of the floral print skirt she was wearing and the swoop-neck silk top that clung to her body. Cyn looked sexy, but not provocative.

"Cyn, where did you get those sandals, they are gorgeous? Are they from Jimmy Choo's latest collection?"

"No. I actually found these online at Zappos," Cyn responded, revealing where she'd gotten her gold wedge-heeled sandals.

The two women were instructed to meet the men on the lower level of the building, so they got into an old elevator. The door closed. A familiar voice from the past spoke, startling the women.

"Hello, Cyndarella," the tall, good-looking man said to his former fiancée.

"Thad!" she spun around and came face-to-face with him as he chuckled. Suddenly, the elevator jolted and came to an abrupt stop, which caused Wiyad and Cyndarella to freeze in their tracks.

"Oh fuck! We're stuck on this damn elevator," Wiyad said, as she began to bang on the doors.

"Afraid that banging won't help," Thad laughed. "Looks like you're stuck with me, after all, Cyndarella! How ironic is that?"

Wiyad quickly sent a text to Bashar that they had arrived and were stuck in the elevator with Cyndarella's ex-fiancé before her device stopped working.

"I've no service on my phone!" Wiyad exclaimed.

"Let me try mine," Cyndarella offered. "Damn it! Mine isn't working either!" She grabbed the emergency phone in the elevator and called for help, but only got a recording when she indicated they were stuck between floors.

"Let me see if I have service," Thad said as he removed his mobile phone from his pocket. Glancing at it, the screen displayed he did have service. Though there was no way he'd tell them. It would be some form of payback for Cyndarella as he knew she was claustrophobic. It would be of satisfaction to witness her meltdown. It messed him up seeing how good she looked! It bought back memories of how insatiable she used to be, until that camel jockey had come along.

"Cyn, you look beautiful as ever! You're living your dream, I see. How many kids did you end up having?"

"That's none of your business," Wiyad spat out at him. She did not like the ravenous way Thad was looking at her cousin's wife.

"It's okay, Wiyad," Cyn said trying to calm the woman down. They were all uncomfortable and she would do just about anything to lighten the mood, so she humored Thad and answered his question. "My husband and I have three children." She spoke softly, while Thad silently glanced at her with scorn.

Wiyad continued to look at her phone and for the fleeting moment she got service. However, it was only long enough to shoot off another text to Bashar that Thad was seriously lusting after his wife and they were in danger.

They could hear some commotion coming outside of the elevator, and knew help was on the way. Thad couldn't help stare at the woman he once thought would carry *his* name and babies with longing and regret. He and his female companions were so caught up at being trapped on the elevator, that they did not feel it began to move.

"Well, I am really happy for you, Cyn. Perhaps if I hadn't have been so selfish, we might have been married ourselves, right now. I still remember how incredible we were together, especially the way you took my love and—"

"Thad! Stop it!" Cyndarella demanded.

Thad relished making the slut pay for leaving him the way she did. It'd taken him a long time to get over her and seeing her again just made him even angrier at her for her past betrayal.

"You're such a tease! You never used to tell me to stop!" he mocked.

"You're a sick motherfucker. You really are," Wiyad responded with disgust. "Fucking pig!"

"That's the very same thing I said about Cyndarella's husband for fucking her while she was wearing my ring!"

"Don't talk to me, you piece of shit!" Wiyad screamed at Thad.

"Damn it, Thad! Enough already! Shut your fucking mouth," Cyn charged back.

Chapter Nineteen

Bashar and Faisal had gotten ahold of someone in Maintenance to help free Wiyad and Cyndarella. Unbeknownst to them, the men heard that last part of their conversation. Bashar's heart raced as he thought of his cousin and wife being jammed into an elevator with Thad. The words he'd spoken to his wife were blatantly immoral. He silently thanked God that Cyn wasn't alone with that man.

Faisal had to do all he could to cool his brother down, but he knew once those doors opened, this Thad guy would pay for disrespecting his sister-in-law. Who in the fuck did he think he was to do something so vile? Bashar threatened to kill him if he'd touched Cyndarella!

The maintenance man finally pried the door opened. Wiyad and Cyndarella jumped off the elevator. Thad was right behind them, checking out Cyndarella's ass. Unfortunately for him, Bashar and Faisal viewed him glancing directly at Cyn's booty, and they confronted the man.

"Who do you think you are? You disrespectful motherfucker! Don't you ever speak to my wife like that again!" Bashar roared, thinking about clocking Thad on his right jaw.

"Oh, so it was okay for you to fuck her when she was my fiancée, huh? Man, you can kiss my ass!" Thad attacked.

The men began exchanging blows in front of a horrified Cyndarella and Wiyad. Bashar and Faisal beat the living shit out of Thad, but he managed to get in a few licks of his own before the security team came to break up the fight. Wiyad threw a kick at Thad's knee while as he was trying to stand up, to Cyn's astonishment.

"Man, if I ever catch you near my wife again!" Bashar yelled.

"Oh my God, Bashar, just stop it! You really hurt him! And your face, you're bleeding!" Cyndarella hollered.

One of the security team intervened. "We need to get a statement from each of you. We'll call the police if either party decides to press charges."

Thad touched his swollen jaw. It hurt like hell, as did his ribs.

"Yeah, call the police. This animal and his cohort attacked me. I should have been the one attacking him because he's the one who stole my—"

"Man, I see you didn't get enough!" Bashar arose again. Cyndarella stepped in front of her husband and finally got him to calm down. The police came and took statements. Thad said he would be consulting with an attorney about pressing charges against Bashar and Faisal.

"You haven't heard the last from me! You messed with the wrong brother," Thad threatened as he walked away. "Goddamn camel jockey scum is all you are!"

Faisal hated that racial slur, just as most Chaldeans did. Right now he had to worry about one: his brother.

"We should have beaten him down some more!" Faisal said. "But he ain't worth no jail time, bro. I think he got the message."

"We're done. Let's get the hell out of here!" Cyndarella proposed as she stormed away from the men, alongside a fuming Wiyad.

Mouna Bazzi took the call from her daughter-in-law and agreed to let the children spend the night at her home, to the relief of Cyndarella. This afternoon seemed like a blur to her, after seeing Bashar and Faisal thumping the living daylights out of Thad. She was pacing back and forth in the kitchen when she heard the garage door open. Bashar was home. She froze in her tracks as her heartbeat started to accelerate when he walked through the door. The look of disgust painted on her face was less than welcoming.

A bruised Bashar walked into the kitchen to find his wife none too pleased with him as he began to talk to her.

"Cyn. I'm sorry that you had to see me and Faisal beat the shit out of that scumbag ex of yours." Cyndarella looked the bruises and scratches on her husband and it made her even more upset.

"You know what, Bashar? You are too old to be trying to catch a case. And the way you and Faisal went at Thad; you could've killed him!"

"Baby, I know that. Wiyad sent text messages saying he was lusting after you, and then Faisal and I overheard what that pig said to you in the elevator and I lost it," Bashar sighed as his shoulders sank.

"I handled it! Thad was being a prick to piss me off, nothing more! That's his style. You beat him really bad, and he is going to press charges against both of you!" Cyn quarreled.

"Our attorneys will make any charges go away. I'm not ever going to let any man disrespect your honor. You know that! I have no regrets, and I'd do it again to teach that fucker a lesson."

An incensed Cyndarella could not believe what she was hearing. She'd always known that her husband would do anything to protect her, but it frightened her to think of how far he might actually go.

"I'm going upstairs," she muttered.

She walked into the den in her bedroom, sat down on the cream leather sectional and took a few deep breaths to calm herself down. She was not pleased when she heard Bashar coming upstairs. He started up again with her.

"Baby, listen. You're mad as hell right now. I understand that, but I will not apologize for defending you. I'm sorry it upset you in doing so, though."

"Me too. I saw a side of you that really scared me, and I, uh, well, I am going to sleep in the guestroom for a while because it totally shook me up."

"Cyndarella, you are not leaving our bedroom! I will sleep on the couch in our den to give you breathing space, but as long as we are married, we sleep in the same bedroom! I don't have to be in bed with you to accomplish that," Bashar appealed.

"Fine! Only if you promise not to touch me!" she shouted, and exited their bedroom before he could respond.

Cyndarella grabbed her keys and left the house. She felt suffocated by Bashar and his demands. His need to control at times didn't usually bother her. But this time, in actuality, he'd managed to tick her the hell off. The enormity of his actions, mixed in with the lack of control he'd displayed earlier, made her nervous. She got into the car and headed out for a drive to get away from her clingy husband.

Chapter Twenty

D enise had a meeting with the national sales managers of several major radio stations this afternoon in her office to discuss the placement of an upcoming media buy for one of Peachtree's clients. Sean was one of the managers who would be coming in. He always teased her about how poised and commanding she could be at work, and what an enticing seductress she was at home.

Natalie ordered lunch from Panera for the meeting. She also set up the conference room where the meeting would take place. Denise was happy that Cyndarella had hired Natalie, a Mexican woman in her mid-fifties who had been downsized by Chrysler, as their administrative assistant.

Natalie was just as meticulous with detail as they were, and she was seasoned with thirty years of experience. She was protective of the staff and knew what was going on with everybody. But she didn't gossip. In the three years since she'd joined them, everything had run smoothly. There were moments when Natalie threw out unexpected zingers and made them all laugh.

The meeting was productive. The national sales managers were all buzzing about the latest soft drink campaign. Media buys were very competitive, and the radio industry was still considered to be highly cutthroat when it came to ad placements. Denise was limited; she'd only be able to select a few stations based on pricing and demographics.

Sean stuck around after the meeting and spent time with Denise in her office, where she managed to get a little work done between the few stolen kisses they shared. Natalie came into her office to give her an overnight package that had arrived.

"Oh, I didn't know you were still hanging with the missus, Sean," Natalie said. "I just wanted to drop off this package."

"Yep. Still here, but I'm about to leave. I have another appointment in Birmingham later on this afternoon," Sean explained.

"It's always great to see a good family man. And you know what? I said I'd wait until I got you two together before I tell you I know how you keep your marriage going!" Natalie mocked. "Your little secret is out of the bag!" she laughed.

"Love, laughter, and sex are our secret, Natalie. Just don't tell anybody," Sean laughed.

"Oh, I won't. But that wasn't what I was referring to, Sean. I've seen your Porsche a couple of times on Saturdays at the Hampton Inn over on Northwestern Drive. You and Denise ain't fooling me! A little love getaway outside of the home ain't never hurt nobody. My Ramon had better get with the program," Natalie sassed, as she walked out of the office.

The woman had become wise to the infidelity of Denise's husband quite by accident. It was amazing what you could learn from getting a manicure. She'd gotten a manicure, alright, but so much more. It was up to Denise to take the ball and run with it now, Natalie thought. She liked Sean a lot, but she believed if a woman was being cheated on, she needed to know about it.

Denise looked at Sean and demanded an explanation.

"Who is the cheap bitch you're having an affair with at the Hampton Inn?"

"I didn't say I was having an affair."

"So, the Saturday afternoons when you're supposedly golfing is a lie, right? You're not at the Hampton Inn? Which is it? Natalie wouldn't lie!"

"I'm not the only man who drives a Porsche. It was somebody else."

"Your vanity license plate is how Natalie knew it was you. It's just she didn't know you were in there fucking someone else! I can call her back in here if you want her to elaborate. It's your call!"

"Dee, let me explain," Sean implored.

"Do I know her? I want to know who the fuck this bitch is!" Denise spat with venom.

"Denise, babe, let me explain. I—" His angry wife cut him off.

"Don't bother. I'll see you at home," Dee replied as tears streamed from her eyes. Sean left, closing the door behind him, wondering if Natalie was being naïve or vindictive in trying to set him up. He knew the disclosure hurt his wife. The only thing he could do was to go home and beg her for forgiveness.

Denise cursed as both her office line and cell phone continued blowing up. She recognized Dr. Shah's phone number and she answered the call.

"Hello."

"Hi there, Denise. It's Dr. Shah. I wanted to personally contact you to say congratulations! You are seven weeks pregnant!" the doctor excitedly informed her. "We need to get you in here A.S.A.P. to do an ultrasound and confirm it." Additionally, he gave her a follow-up appointment and told to discontinue the Clomid, and he'd call in a prescription for prenatal vitamins for her.

Denise sat shocked and dismayed about her pregnancy. The enthusiasm she thought she would feel proved to be nonexistent. She *could* not tell Sean about this baby until she decided what she wanted to do about their marriage. A baby wouldn't keep them together. She preferred him to leave her, rather than stay out of obligation because they had another baby on the way.

Work would be the way out for her, she thought as she left to go home. She needed time to devise an exit plan without involving her husband. Time wasn't on her side. She would have to give the performance of her life to maintain her pregnancy and sanity while keeping her unsuspecting husband and daughter at bay and in the dark until she was ready to make the big reveal.

Chapter Twenty-One

Vette became depressed when she learned about Tavie and Orville's engagement, but she was determined to get a head start on bridal shower venues that she could discuss with her friends. Louis noticed his girlfriend was not her usual bubbly self, and mentioned it to her, and she was honest with him and told her she was tired of faking that she was happy when things seemed up in the air about their own future.

Vette called Tavie to find out how far she'd gotten with her wedding plans in the last week, but she had not heard back from her. She decided to give Tavie another call and give her a piece of her mind for not returning her phone call.

"Hey, Vette," Tavie said almost in a whisper like tone.

"What's going on, girl? I've been trying to reach you. I'd like to start planning the bridal shower."

"Vette, a shower won't be necessary. There isn't going to be a wedding."

"What?" Vette's voice rose as she questioned her friend. "What the hell happened?" Tavie remained silent, worrying her friend.

"Tavie? Are you still there?" Vette asked. She heard her friend sniffling quietly.

"I'm here," Tavie uttered almost inaudibly.

"Hang up the phone and pull yourself together, girl. It'll be all right. I am on my way."

"Okay."

Vette hadn't a clue to the reason why her friend had called off her engagement. Tavie had been so elated preparing for her future with Orville. Vette wanted to call Denise and Cyndarella to see if they knew anything, but she opted to wait until she'd met with Tavie. She didn't want to put Tavie's business out there, unless Tavie wanted it known.

Tavie spilled everything to Vette as they sipped on Starbuck's soy skinny lattes. Vette had arrived and seen Tavie was in a bad way. It didn't look like she'd bathed or combed her hair in days. Vette went into the bedroom to pull out a pair of jeans and a tank top for her friend, and told her she needed to shower as she was getting her out for some much needed fresh air.

Vette could not believe Orville had continued getting the goods from his ex-wife after they split. It didn't make sense, but Orville had confirmed to his fiancée that everything was true, except he was unsure about the child being his.

"He said he is going to get a paternity test for the boy to see if he is his."

"What if he isn't his son, Tavie? Can you forgive him and move forward?"

"He was still sleeping with Geneva and me at the same time! And afterwards! He probably is his son. I'm not going to deal with it!" she scoffed.

"Girl, I don't blame you at all, but you *have* to deal with this. Orville was wrong, but Geneva did say they were no longer messing around. Maybe you two can get counseling and try to make it work. If truth be told, he appears rather taken with you."

"If that were the case, we wouldn't be in this situation, Vette, now, would we? I am going to counseling alright, but for myself right now." Tavie shook her head as she continued with the conversation. "I think there something wrong with how I choose the men in my life. It's a pattern of deceitful lies and I'm tired of it."

Vette began to appreciate her relationship with Louis even more. He hadn't proposed, but she could answer his home or cell phone and check his text messages. He appeared on the up and up and had nothing to hide. Louis was good to her, and now she began to wonder if she truly needed a ring of bling on her finger.

"Orville seems to really be in love with you. I wouldn't get rid of him altogether. Give it some time."

"I got rid of Mack. He begged me for a second chance!"

"He was a dog!"

"Granted, but who's worse? I chose Orville instead, even though he was still legally married to Geneva, though separated. Mack and I were so close to having something real for once. I just was too scared to trust him or the feelings that I felt."

"You've got to stop being down on yourself," Vette suggested. "You would have been a fool to not be afraid after what Mack put you through."

"The only reason I got with Orville initially was to get revenge on Geneva for cheating with Mack. Our relationship caught us both by surprise."

"Whatever happened to Mack-daddy?" Vette inquired.

"We don't keep in touch anymore. I haven't seen him in ages, since I switched school systems. I heard he was dating this labor relations chick from the Teachers' Union."

Tavie consented to letting Vette tell the others about the wedding cancellation. Vette would do a good job of sharing everything they needed to know. Moreover, Vette found a new lease of appreciating what she had, versus something she might never be able to obtain.

A phone call interrupted the dinner date the gentleman was having. A recognizable phone number flashed across his screen. Hesitantly, he paused momentarily before taking the call.

"Hey, stranger," Mack said. Geneva proceeded to fill Mack in on how she put Tavie on blast. She also told him something that was definitely news to him: Orville Kirkland was indeed the father of her son, and Tavie wasn't happy about it.

"Is she alright?" Mack asked with genuine concern.

"How in the hell would I know? That's for you to find out! Goodbye, Mackenzie!" Geneva chirped.

"What was that about?" Brenda Barker, the current woman in his life, asked.

"Nothing I can't handle," he replied.

Octavia Slade had scarred him in a way no other woman had. He'd taken her for granted, parading other women around her, and she'd left him for a Jamaican! He thought they'd be together forever, but she couldn't trust him, nor was she willing to put any more work into the long relationship that they'd had.

Mack saw the Instagram pictures posted of her on vacation in Jamaica with the Rasta man, and he'd felt a pang of jealousy because Tavie had chosen Orville over him. He also saw her engagement announcement pictures posted on Facebook, where they still were friends. They just didn't correspond with one another anymore. It was too awkward.

Chapter Twenty-Two

D r. Margaret Wiener listened to the distraught woman disclose the nature of her visit. She was in agreement that this lady, a single woman and teacher by profession, needed therapy. Because Octavia Slade was a new patient, she'd have to ask her preliminary intake questions that would help in upcoming counseling sessions.

"Octavia, how often do you speak to your fiancé, Orville?"

"A couple times a week, briefly. I don't want to talk to him," Tavie answered.

"And by not really talking to him, what does that accomplish?" the doctor probed further.

"Nothing, I guess. I just don't want to see his face, or hear his voice, that's all! Is that a crime?"

"Of course not! Has he said anything in his defense for his actions?"

"He confessed, you know. Said he was sorry, and all." Tavie exhaled noisily. "Orville wants to work things out."

"What do you want?" Dr. Wiener inquired, and Tavie laughed sarcastically.

"I don't know. I can't even see how it would matter at this point."

"Indeed, Octavia, it does matter. First, can you tell me why was it so easy for you to accept your nemesis' word as being the truth, knowing your history? She's slept with your fiancé and ex-boyfriend. Didn't you find that odd, or suspicious?"

"I did. I had no idea they were still having sex, Dr. Wiener! When my loving fiancé confirmed he was still fucking his ex-wife back then, I was done," Tavie flippantly retorted.

"Octavia, we have a few more minutes before we wrap up. I like to see you again, sometime next week if it possible." Tavie nodded her head in agreement.

"Just give me a day and time and I'll be here."

"I'd like you to have another visit with me before you meet with your fiancé, because you do have to face him. I'd also like to discuss your ex-boyfriend, Mack."

Chapter Twenty-Three

T avie felt good talking about her problems to a stranger. Her parents had been supportive of the decision she'd made in foregoing the wedding. They were disappointed, yet were able to provide her with comfort that she'd made the best decision her life. Her mother said that until the paternity test results came back, there was no way she and Orville could move forward.

The task of checking email was something Tavie tried to do at least a couple of times a week. She looked in her inbox, and an item immediately caught her eye. Cautiously she clicked on the email.

Tavie,

I hope this email finds you well. I wanted to let you know Geneva called me and gloated about spilling her guts to you in relation to your engagement with Orville, and I am concerned. I will reach out to you in a couple of days by phone to make sure you're okay. All my best to you.

Mackenzie Dooley

Tavie reread the message several times. He'd sent the email a couple of days ago. She had the same phone number as when they'd been together, but she wasn't sure if she wanted to talk to him. Surely *he* had to be gloating about the breakup! He couldn't stand Orville or Geneva. He felt Geneva manipulated everyone, and he'd washed his hands of her.

Looking through her contacts, Tavie indeed still had Mack's phone number. The least she could do was call him to thank him for the kind words. She hoped he would be too occupied elsewhere to take her call if she reached out to him at home instead of on his cell phone. She dialed his number and his reply startled her.

"Octavia? I can't believe you still have my number."

"Hello, Mackenzie. It used to be *our* number, remember?" The conversation momentarily came to a halt before Mack responded.

"Tavie, of course I remember," he softly acknowledged. "Geneva called me last week bragging about all the bullshit she dumped on you. I'm sorry you have to deal with this."

"Me too," she sighed.

"Can I see you? Lunch, dinner, whatever you want?"

"Mack, I don't think it's a good time for me, right now. I'm going through a lot. I need to be by myself."

"Woman, you sound awful. I know you could use a friend right now. So am I coming out to Auburn Hills to pick you up, or are you coming here?"

The two hung up after agreeing to meet for dinner on Saturday. Tavie hadn't the foggiest idea why she said yes. What could seeing the man accomplish? Hell, she thought, he was to a degree the cause of why she'd landed in this quandary. Mack sent her a text later saying it was good to hear her voice, and simple as the message was, it made her smile for the first time in weeks.

Chapter Twenty-Four

"Set it up over here, please," Willa Worthy directed the bounce house delivery team. She'd rented a Batman inflatable bounce house for all the children who would be in attendance today, as well as a face painter and magician. The party rental vendor had arrived earlier to set up the backyard with tables and chairs to seat their guests.

Most of the invited guests either had children or grandchildren like her, and the kids needed to be entertained just as the adults did. Willa, being a retired librarian, believed that children needed to stay busy and active. If they didn't, everyone would pay the price of their boredom.

Vibrant, beautiful blue and white hydrangeas and red rose bushes were spread out over the Worthys' backyard. Cyn's parents had updated their landscaping, and outfitted the two-tiered deck with new Martha Stewart patio furniture. Vernon Worthy had a custom-made charcoal grill tailored to his specifications that had 2,000 square feet of cooking space. In addition the grill included a built-in smoker that made their neighbors jealous when they caught a whiff of the apple woodchips stinking up the neighborhood.

Willa Worthy held her annual garden party and each year it got bigger. They actually hired a rental company to set up their entire backyard with tables and chairs. The patio furniture, albeit quite fashionable, was not enough to accommodate the crowd they were anticipating.

As the morning progressed, Willa tended to minor details with the caterer during a phone call, and after hanging up she felt a great sense of relief in knowing that she would have waiters staffing her event during a three-hour window. Pete, Bashar and Vernon took care of supplying all the liquor and mixers the bartender needed to have on hand to whip up a slew of invigorating summer drinks for the crowd.

Willa dressed in a Topshop floral dress with a white pair of flat Ann Klein strappy sandals. She'd gotten her hair freshly cut and flat-ironed it into a sleek chin-length hairstyle with bangs. Vernon had changed into a pair of light gray Bermuda shorts, teamed with a Michael Kors two-pocket white linen shirt. He also wore his favorite pair of Sperry shoes that he swore by because they were extremely comfortable.

As the guests arrived, the Worthy family was delighted to see their former daughter-in-law, who'd flown in for the festivities from Minneapolis. Julia made no secret about her desire to reunite with Pete, though he'd moved back to Michigan, but they still had a lot of work ahead of them, because neither Vernon nor she thought they would be capable of it.

"There's nothing like a good party!" Vette called out to the guests.

Cyn and Bashar, along with their kids, arrived in time to hear Vette's declaration as she mingled.

"Hey Vette? What's up?" Cyn asked. "Mom and Dad got a house full. We had to park way down the street!"

"Hell, I know. I did too, but it's worth it, girl. This is so nice! It gets bigger every year."

"I've been here all week helping Pete and Pops get everything set up so it wouldn't be so much work on them," Bashar added. "Mr. Worthy has always been like a second father to me."

"You're like a son to him, too. I'm so glad that you have such a strong relationship. I think Pete is a wee bit jealous," Cyn kidded.

"Speaking of Pete, man, he looks handsome today, Cyn. *Real* handsome!"

"Oh shit," Bashar laughed. "Louis better watch his back!"

"He sure better," Vette agreed as she walked off in the direction of Pete Worthy. "And he better hurry up and bring his ass over here before I get into some trouble."

Cyn wondered if Vette still was crushing on her brother. It was humorous to her, but they were older now, and she was concerned for a vulnerable Vette who appeared to be losing her patience with Louis.

"I hope Louis hurry up and proposes to Corvette," Cyn spoke, as Tavie and Denise walked up to them.

"Marriage ain't what it seems, so maybe she's better off waiting until it's right for them," Denise theorized, without truly explaining how she'd personally come to that conclusion.

"Sean still under the weather, I see?" Bashar asked.

"Afraid so. I'm not going to stay long. I just wanted to see everyone for a bit, and let Marla have a good time. I feel like I'm coming down with something too," Dee replied.

As the friends mingled and huddled in conversation, they accepted drinks from the servers who came around periodically to remove their glasses, in exchange for new one. Denise couldn't help spying on Vette, who was acting like a schoolgirl around Pete. He brought back memories that only the two of them shared, and seeing Vette so captivated by him did make her green with envy. Apparently, she wasn't the only one, as Julia approached them.

"Your little friend over there is all but perched on top of Pete's pecker right now," she huffed to Cyndarella. "What's her deal?"

"Alcohol is her deal, Julia. You don't have anything to worry about."

"She really is harmless," Tavie said to the brown-skinned, hazel-eyed, curvaceous woman wearing a cool blue and white polka dot dress.

"Ain't no woman with a vagina who's harmless, unless she's happy with a man of her own! Does she have one by the way?" Julia asked.

"Yes, and there he is! Hey, Louis," Bashar called out, and the man walked over to greet them.

"Where's my love?" he asked, as he sipped on a glass of Prosecco.

"Standing at the food table, next to *my love*," Julia said, pointing at the pair who looked as if they were on a date. "I better rescue him if I plan to hang onto him!"

Julia walked off and marched over to where Pete was holding court with Vette, linked her arm into his and through clenched teeth spoke to the smitten woman.

"I came to claim my man, and I suggest you do the same. Louis, is it?" she asked pointing once again in her friend's direction. Vette was startled to see Louis, but she wasn't going to let Julia get at her.

"Julia, I'm glad you met Louis. He is the love of my life. Pete, he's my best friend's brother whom I've known way longer than you. No reason to be envious. It's not like we're held up somewhere in a cockpit!" Vette snapped, and she made her point based on the look on Julia's face. "Excuse me, you two," she said, placing her drink down and proceeding to walk away.

"I can see why he cheated on her! She is a major bitch!" Vette said, as she welcomed Louis to the party. "Hey, baby."

"She's feeling insecure, Vette. Try to stay away from her if you can. She's sensitive."

"No shit!" Vette fumed. "I was actually telling Pete he should take her back, but now I'm not so sure."

"Well, that's up to them to figure out, dear. They don't need any interference," Louis spoke, as the others nodded their heads in agreement. Louis excelled at everything he set his mind to, and Vette was one of those things. He'd be damned if he'd let her get away from him. He knew he hadn't completely given her the commitment she'd wanted and, furthermore, deserved. Pete Worthy was a threat to their relationship, though he couldn't really blame Pete because he seemed like he was glad to be rescued by his ex-wife, and Corvette looked as if she felt all alone.

CYNDARELLA AND BASHAR stayed to assist her parents clean up after the party. The servers helped store all the food into containers so that her parents would have food for days, in addition to giving some to the homeless shelter in the area. The children couldn't hang, and fell asleep inside the house with their grandmother. Tonight had been a major success, for yet another year.

"We're going to have to take this over for your parents soon, Cyn."

"I know."

"We can approach them about it next year. It's a major event in the subdivision."

"They do such a good job organizing it. Thank God they finally let us pay for the food!" she said.

"We're paying for everything from now on. I'm insisting on it!"

"That's why love you, Baz! You're so thoughtful!"

The exhausted couple finished tearing down the party favors, and ended the night at the Worthys', where they spent the night with the children in the guest room.

Chapter Twenty-Five

"This is some *bullshit*. You won't even to talk to me! We can't go on like this, Denise," Sean tried to appeal to his nonchalant wife. "You barely look at me, and this hostility is not good for Marla".

"Oh, so you now you're concerned about what's good for Marla?" she sulked. "Fucking hypocrite!" she fired back.

Things had been strained between the couple for the past few weeks. They had reached their breaking point. Denise and Sean had legitimate grounds for feeling each had betrayed the other and both wondered if the marriage was worth salvaging.

"You asked me to give you space. I have. I even missed the Worthys' garden party. *You* know how much I enjoy *that* party! I'm really tired of you calling the shots around here, Denise, to be honest with you."

"What the hell do you know about being honest, huh, Sean? Marla and I are leaving for San Diego on Saturday. I will be working onsite at Peachtree's affiliate agency, Latitude Worldwide, on the beverage account. Marla will be going to camp there while I am working."

"How long will you be gone?"

"Three weeks, give or take. We'll be back in time for Marla to get ready for school," Denise clarified for Sean, who sat down on the black leather loveseat next to his wife.

"I don't think a break is what we need right now. We need to deal with this crisis head-on."

"I really don't care what you think! I'm leaving. We can deal with whatever a farce of a marriage we have when I return," Denise resolved.

"It's pretty obvious. You couldn't care less about what *I* have to say, period. This sick need for control you have is the reason why *our* marriage is crumbling. I think it's time for us both to seek legal counsel to make out what our options are," Sean determined.

"Oh, I see. Your little whore's pussy must be real good to make you talk some shit like that to me!"

Sean ignored his wife's comments, and grabbed his gym bag and went to work out.

The very presence of Sean distressed Denise, for it stood as a constant reminder that he'd cheated on her with another married woman and humiliated her in a public way. The nausea she had was even more prevalent when he was around, and she didn't know if it was because of the pregnancy or her nerves. She was ten weeks pregnant, and she had no immediate plans of sharing the news of the impending birth with Sean.

This second pregnancy was a lot gentler on her than the first had been. She had less weight gain but more morning sickness, which she hid from her co-workers and Sean, who had recently been sleeping in their basement guestroom.

Denise was shaken by this latest verbal altercation with Sean. He clearly wanted a divorce. She wanted to talk to him, but was terrified that she'd reveal too much, particularly about the pregnancy. She could not afford to lose control, even if it meant that she appeared obstinate. They were in no position to bring another baby into their broken relationship. She'd get a lawyer and have Sean served before he had her served. If he wanted out, damn it, she'd give him what he wanted! He didn't deserve her anyway.

Denise had spoken to Cyndarella about working at their affiliate office, which Cyn was fine with. She even recommended the camp for Marla. Cyndarella had no idea that Denise was pregnant and she hated keeping that from her friend, but sometimes, you need to keep some things to yourself, especially when you didn't want to hear, let alone take someone else's advice.

Chapter Twenty-Six

Vette looked out of the kitchen window while she waited on her morning cup of coffee. The children were staying with their Aunt Courtney and her brother-in-law, Bob. Her older sister had had several miscarriages, and after a while, she and Bob had decided to stop trying. Tara didn't offer much solace by telling Courtney that "babies choose who they want as parents, and then God makes it happen." Courtney adored the children, and she and Bob decided they might try to adopt some of their own.

The sound of footsteps could be heard coming from upstairs. Louis was awake. They'd attended a retirement party for one of his friends who was a judge. It had gone well, until Karolyn, a friend of his ex-wife, had deliberately ignored her, and kept talking about people and events Vette had no knowledge of. It had been fifteen minutes of 'remember when' madness that was uncomfortable, and had made her feel ill at ease. She'd taken out her phone and begun texting her friends, which was something she hardly ever did while out. It had taken that for Louis to steer the conversation to current topics to include his woman.

Thoughts of Peter Worthy had embedded themselves in her mind. The man looked and smelled good! And he was single again; despite the obvious fact Julia wanted him back. She didn't blame Julia for cheating on Pete because he had player written all over him, especially when he came up from Minneapolis to Detroit.

Cyndarella said her dog of a brother had a line of hoes waiting on him at his beck and call. It stopped the siblings from being as close as they once had been. Julia was an extremely pleasant woman, and she was glad to see that her friendliness did not make her a pushover for his foolishness. Vette had a newfound meaning for the word cockpit, after hearing how flight attendant Julia's affair with a pilot, no less, had become exposed after work one day. Game recognized game all day!

"Good morning, sunshine! You look like you were miles away. What were you thinking about?" Louis asked.

"Good morning to you! I was actually thinking about how you subtly took up for me last night when that witch excluded me out of the conversation. I hate that you still share friends with your ex, but I understand," she sighed.

"Babe, I will always make sure you're okay. Karolyn is just Karolyn! Don't let her get to you."

"I'm trying. It seems like she's everywhere we go, though. I tell you, she's still spying on you for Jacquelyn, and you know it!"

"I love it when you speak your truth, my dear. So let me speak my truth: let's go back to bed," Louis snaked his arm around Vette's back, but she had to gently decline.

"I can't. I have a deposition that I gotta get to. Rain check, baby, okay? I will make it up to you later".

"Damn straight you will!" he shot back, while giving her a playful slap on her ass.

Chapter Twenty-Seven

P F Chang's had its usual dinner crowd, and Tavie was glad that she had gotten to the Troy restaurant a half hour earlier than needed to get seated. She had a drink at the bar and made small talk with some of the patrons as they bonded over the Detroit Tigers and Chicago Whitesox game. The Tigers were beating the Whitesox 5-0 in the seventh inning, to the delight of the crowd. Mack had left her a voicemail to say that he was on his way, and she'd sent him a text when she'd arrived at the parking lot.

The pager alert went off, allowing her to be seated, and she ordered another drink. She felt extremely ill at ease presently. A part of her did not want to be there, but her curiosity had gotten the better of her. This wasn't about her seeing an old flame. It was more about him spilling the tea on all he'd been told by Geneva. She felt like she needed to know more.

"Hey, love. How you doing? Give me a hug girl," her former lover spoke, startling her.

"Mackenzie, hello!" she said, as they shared an embrace while checking each other out.

"Octavia, it's really good to see you! Tell me what's going on since we last talked?" Mack asked, while taking in the sight of his ex-girlfriend. She was still as attractive and desirable as he remembered. He was willing himself not to stare at her, but she made it hard wearing that tight, white tank top with a white denim vest and a silver multi-layered necklace that crested softly on her small breasts. She'd gained a few pounds, though he wouldn't dare mention that to her; he thought she looked healthier than when she'd had her previous smaller frame.

"Not a lot has been going on. Orville went to the lab last week for the DNA test. I just don't want to see him before the results are through."

"Aren't you supposed to be planning your happily ever after? You can't let this get in your way if this relationship is something you really want."

"And deal with Geneva for the rest of my life? Speaking of the witch, what did she say about me?" Tavie asked.

"Nothing more than what I told you before. She got to you. That appeared to be her main goal. So, is your wedding going to happen or what?" Mack could see Tavie appeared apprehensive while she rambled.

"I don't know. It was going to be informal, nothing fancy, you know? Right before school started back. I ask myself how could there be a wedding when Orville was still boning Geneva before, during and after the divorce! Now a kid?" Tavie shook her head in despair.

"Octavia, you knew what his status was when you hooked up with him, but that didn't stop you then from wanting to be with him."

"Oh, so I'm supposed to give him a pass on cheating on me?" A temporary intrusion stopped Mack from answering her for a moment

The waiter took their order of sesame chicken, which they'd both ordered with brown rice, along with a couple glasses of Pinot Grigio. Mack sensed Tavie's heightened anxiety as she twisted her silver necklace around her fingers.

"Octavia, what Orville did was wrong. But if he's been exclusive with you for a couple of years, can't you cut him some slack and forgive the man?" Mack inquired. "Look I saw those pictures of you in Jamaica on Facebook, and you both looked like you were madly in love."

"Oh, I didn't know you saw those, Mackenzie," Tavie, said shifting uncomfortably in her chair.

"I'm glad you found someone to share your life with. Your happiness is important, no matter who you decide to be with. In every relationship, Tavie, there are always going to be challenges you have to deal with. You know that whole for better or worse stuff?"

"Wow, so you're my therapist now? How in the hell did that happen?" she laughed. "But seriously, I know you're right. I *want* to be happily married someday, but it seems to elude me."

The waiter returned with their main course, temporarily interrupting their conversation.

"Mack, I must be doing something wrong to keep drawing these *losers* to me! I mean, this scenario keeps occurring on some level, but with a different cast of characters," Tavie reflected, as Mack winced at her words.

"I was one of those *losers*, remember? If I can speak for myself, you were not the problem. It was my ego that caused us to fall apart and you to distrust me. We're over, but you still have to sort through this Orville shit. Does that make sense?"

Tavie shook her head in agreement. "I didn't mean to offend you."

"You didn't. Just stop blaming yourself for other people's mishaps."

"I'm going to a therapist now. She is really analytical, but very thorough."

"If you need me to come to one of your visits to shed light on our past, I'm willing to do that for you, if it will help," Mack offered to a somewhat astonished Tavie.

"Thank you for offering to do that for me, Mr. Dooley."

"Correction, dear. It's Dr. Dooley, now," he bragged. "I got my PhD back in 2011."

"Congratulations, to you, Dr. Dooley! But all kidding aside, thanks for being here for me. More than anything I need to sort through this mess and figure it out, or return my damn gown! It is so beautiful, but at the rate I'm going, I may never get a chance to wear it!" Tavie shared candidly, as tears made their way down her cheeks.

"Octavia, you will wear your wedding gown someday. I don't know when, but I promise you, it will happen," he guaranteed.

"You really think so?"

"Without question."

Mack comforted Tavie over a cup of cappuccino after their meal. Tavie saw a humbled man this evening. She thought never in her lifetime she'd witness such a change in Mack. He was still good-looking, but extremely reserved. Though he made it clear that they were over, she felt a pang of sadness as their evening came to an end.

Mack had arrived this evening without any pretense or expectations, other than to make sure Tavie was okay. His sister Jade occasionally kept in touch with Tavie. She had actually been the source who'd alerted him about Tavie's vacation pictures when they were posted up on Facebook and Instagram. He regretted looking at the intimate and cozy photos of Tavie and that dreadlocked, long-faced Jamaican Rasta man who she had left him for.

For a short while, they had rekindled their relationship before Tavie had decided to get involved again with Orville and completely shut him out. He couldn't reason with her, as her justification was he'd cheated with Geneva. They went back and forth for months, but he knew that they were caput.

The night hadn't been a total bust for Mack, even though seeing Tavie's anguish over Orville stung like a bee. And the fact that she could ever blame herself for brothers fucking around on her personally embarrassed him for the role he'd played in making her come to that erroneous conclusion. He meant what he said about being available to meet with the therapist so he could shed light on the situation.

Chapter Twenty-Eight

"Before we began our session today, I'd like to share with you that each of my patients start off with a blank canvas. Your willingness to be honest determines how vivid that canvas's colors will be."

Tavie was wowed by Dr. Wiener's analogy. It created a powerful image in her mind while she focused on her therapy session. Dr. Wiener was ready to start.

"So tell me Octavia, what is going on between you and Orville?"

"Stalled. He took a DNA test and he's waiting to hear back from the lab."

"What do you mean when you say things are stalled?" Dr. Wiener inquired of an uneasy Tavie, who sat with slumped shoulders slouching down in an oversized chair.

"Until we know the results of the paternity test, I can't make a decision on our future together."

"Are you basing your decision solely on whether or not Orville is determined to be the father of this young boy, in relation to your future?" the doctor pressed on for clarification.

"Orville had an affair with his ex-wife and repeatedly lied to me about having any other women in his life other than me," Tavie puffed.

"It doesn't sound like this is an appropriate time for you to be making future plans, Octavia. Do you agree?"

"Yes I do. Besides, I don't trust Orville any more. He came at me so hard, that's really why I gave in. He was my accidental lover."

"What does that mean?" a perplexed Dr. Wiener asked.

Tavie recognized she'd previously only given a partial explanation of the backdrop surrounding Orville, Geneva and her former boyfriend, Mack, and how their lives intertwined with one another's. She explained how she'd stumbled upon Geneva and the very fact she was Orville's wife when she'd found him and her watching the sex tape Tavie and Orville had made as foreplay. Furthermore, she revealed to Dr. Wiener the timing of the unplanned pregnancy and subsequent miscarriage which had helped unravel the previous relationship with Mack.

"Octavia, pursuing a relationship like this was not only a risk, but toxic. Why did you choose it?"

"I stopped seeing Orville for a couple of months, and then he told me he was moving to Saginaw and he wanted to say goodbye. I confronted him. He explained the two of them had married young and had an open relationship, but they had decided to end it."

"What made you believe him?"

Frustration seeped into Tavie's voice as she provided the answers to the questions Dr. Wiener was interrogating her with.

"This might sound crazy, but it was never about Orville. I wanted to get revenge on Geneva by fucking her husband, so she could see how it felt to mess with someone's man!" she spewed out.

"But how would that make sense if they were planning on ending their relationship, Octavia? Let's shift gears for a minute. Tell me about Mack."

Tavie discussed the ups and downs of her previous relationship with Mack, in that was fraught with problems. She'd literally jumped from the frying pan into the fire, which was why she found herself mentally burnt to a crisp at this moment in time. It was the next admission that surprised the therapist.

"Mack agreed to come see me on your behalf? What prompted that decision?"

"I blame myself for being a magnet for attracting the wrong men, and all. He offered to clarify the part he played in our relationship."

"By all means, I'd like for him to schedule an appointment to discuss this further."

"Do you want him to come to my next session?" Tavie asked.

"No. Have him give the office a call," Dr. Wiener stipulated. "It is time for you to meet with Orville, but please do so in a public place. I'd like you to arrange this before your next appointment if possible."

After Octavia left her office, Dr. Wiener felt the woman was very troubled and headed for a nervous breakdown. She seemed to be obsessed with controlling men, and revenge, and that drove her to make warped choices. Interestingly enough, this Mack individual could be crucial in the outcome of her patient's therapy. The sooner he called, the better.

Chapter Twenty-Nine

"D ear God! This place is magnificent!" Mouna Bazzi exclaimed. "It sure is," Willa Worthy agreed.

It was a long three-and-a-half-hour drive, but Cyndarella took a carload of family with her to get a little rest and relaxation up north at the lakefront community of South Haven, Michigan. The new construction upscale home belonged to Ephraim Vanderbilt, of Vanderbilt homes. The Vanderbilts were close family friends of the Bazzis.

The home housed enough sleeping space for up to ten people. She had seven with her, minus her husband. Bashar was not happy with his wife's spur of the moment decision to whisk the family away without him, and he gave her a piece of his mind. Faisal was not thrilled either that his wife, Samira, bailed on him as well with their kids. Wiyad was mad at Cyndarella and Samira for making such a big deal out of the situation and did not want to go on the trip with them.

Cyndarella had contemplated allowing her husband back into their bed, but that went out the window when Thad's attorney served them with a subpoena for medical bills, plus pain and suffering. Bashar started up talking shit again because Thad wanted $25,000 in damages, but Faisal and Bashar's attorney settled for $15,000 to make the case go away. That was an expensive ass-whipping, which didn't have to have happened, and she'd let him have it. She promised to call him to let him know when they arrived so he wouldn't have a fit.

Stunning Lake Michigan views mesmerized the family from the first and second floors, creating tranquility throughout the vacation home.

"Mommy, Mommy, look!" Zahir screamed with excitement, gaining his mother's attention.

"Now, Mommy!" Zaid, his twin, ran towards his mother, tugging at her arm to bring her into what was to be the twins' bedroom, along with their four-year-old cousin, Wally.

The kid-friendly bedroom was decorated with four built-in bead-board beds. Two were on each side, with nautical ship lights for reading and story time before bed.

"Oh my goodness," Cyndarella chimed in. "Boys, this is really lovely, but you have got to keep it neat and clean. Do you understand me?"

"Yes, Mommy," the boys responded in unison.

"Yes, for me too, Auntie Cyn," her pint-sized, cleft-chinned nephew, Wally, said.

Cyndarella helped the boys as they negotiated which bed each wanted without any major problems. Although the boys got along well, at times, they had problems with sharing their things with one another, and it was no different for Wally, who was younger than his eight-year-old sister, Leylah. After unpacking and sorting their belongings, they went to join the others.

Nadia and Leylah had not made it up to their room. They were checking out the finished basement that included a Ping-Pong table and massive flat screen television, surrounded by a cozy seating area. Cyndarella managed to gather the girls, got them settled in and, for the second time, attempted to join her family who were gathered outside on the front porch.

In a half-hour, her mother-in-law had made a huge pitcher of fresh blueberry lemonade, which was one of her favorite summer drinks. It was literally lemons, fresh lime and at least a pint of blueberries that Mouna poured into the concoction, and it was heavenly. They weren't hungry because they'd stopped along the way, but they did come prepared with their own groceries.

Mouna handed Cyndarella a glass of lemonade.

"Here you are, beautiful! Thanks for bringing us up here." Mouna embraced her before handing her the cold drink.

"You are welcome, Ma Bazzi. We are going to have a blast!"

There was a resounding chant from the group of 'yes!' The midsummer record heat wave had made headlines this year. However, the close proximity to Lake Michigan helped cool off the area with gentle summer breezes, as they sat on Adirondack chairs watching the waves.

Cyndarella and Samira walked down to the private beach so the children could swim and build sandcastles in the afternoon, while Mouna and Willa stayed back at the house to prepare their dinner. The women had gotten to be friends after their children's wedding, to the surprise of Bashar and his wife. The acceptance of their families made their union stronger.

Cyndarella was wearing a navy bikini, with a matching cover-up, along with a pair of sunglasses. She'd pulled her hair back in a ponytail because in the heat it was hard to want to do anything else. Samira had a short, layered haircut, as she said that she felt that because she had gained weight with her children she didn't feel attractive with longer hair. She convinced herself into believing that the shorter cut made her look thinner.

It was evident that Samira had lost a couple of pounds and Cyndarella let her know that she thought she looked great in her floral one-piece bathing suit.

"Samira, you lost weight. Good for you. Did you go on the Atkins Diet like you planned?"

"No. I bought all these books, with all these meal plans, and I couldn't do it. The induction phase I couldn't get through, you know? I went to Weight Watchers instead."

"Wow! So you have to count points instead?"

"Yeah, but there are so many food choices to choose from, Cyndarella! And I'm never hungry. Do you hear me? Never!" Samira emphasized.

"Are you going to be okay this week, or do we need to go out to get you anything?"

"Nope. We're good. I give myself some room for times like these, and still eat healthy, but get back on track when I go home. How do you always stay so damn slim?" Samira laughed.

"Do you really have to ask? Girl, it's work and my damn kids!"

"I know they are a handful. So you're still on strike with Bashar, huh?" Samira asked a relaxed Cyndarella, as they continued lying out on the beach.

"Hell yeah, and unfortunately everybody probably knows about it by now, even my dad and brother!" Cyn's voice filled with exasperation. "I thought you were on strike, too. When did you give in?"

"I get so turned on when Faisal begs, even when I am mad at him. I haven't totally given in to him, though. I give in long enough to come, and then I move away from him and tell him I'm not in the mood. It frustrates him because he ends up jacking off."

"Oooh, they are so getting what they deserve!" The women laughed in agreement.

"Finally, my cousin is *so* fucking happy after everything he's been through. I don't think he will ever forget that horrible time back in Iraq." Samira shuddered at the thought.

"He can't forget it. He tries to make sense of it, but things just don't add up, and it bothers him and me too. Having the kids has helped him to move beyond it."

Chapter Thirty

Samira shook her head in repugnance at the thought of Bashar's confinement, as Cyndarella watched with empathy. How hard must it have been for her cousin who barely recognized his own life once he was freed, only to have to lose the one thing that kept him sane while he was away, though that was beside the point now. Bashar got the bronze-skinned, brown-eyed, voluptuous beauty in the end, and his family couldn't have been happier for it, Samira thought, as she looked at the woman before her with respect and admiration.

"You know what, Cyn? I am so glad that you two found your way back to each other and you are officially a part of our family. I couldn't imagine you not being a part of our lives. It wasn't easy, I know, with the whole race thing and all. Are you okay talking about it?" Samira wanted to tread carefully on the sensitive subject, in spite of the fact previously they have had such discussions.

"Being a part of this crazy family means a lot to me too. I can truly attest to the fact I stumbled onto my relationship with Bashar by chance," Cyn reminisced. "He was relentless in his pursuit of me, and I was the one who brought up the whole race thing. Even back then, you didn't see many Chaldean men dating any women other than their own, unless they were looking to get laid."

"And we're not supposed to openly date until we are engaged, or about to be engaged. Our families would have a stroke if one of us were caught. But that has drastically changed for the better," Samira suggested. "I think it was always you for him. The only other girl I knew who was nuts over him was Manal Delly and he never gave her the time of day. Your children are the best and they are so well adjusted. You've done a good job in raising them to know who they are. More of our men are marrying Americans now."

"Uh, cuz, you don't need to tell me that! Every time one of the so-called cousins or friends gets serious about an American woman, they summon me to meet them for my opinion," Cyn scoffed. "Bashar was the only Chaldean man I dated, ever! I don't have much to tell them, other than they need to get on the best way they can."

"*Really*?" Samira asked with an astonished tone.

"You sound surprised, though you shouldn't be. What I had with Thad was not the best relationship, and I didn't want a repeat."

"That's understandable. Your ex-fiancé was Black, right? Wiyad said he was a looker but couldn't keep his eyes off you, even though he tormented you in the elevator. Now all the Chaldean men want to finish where Faisal and Bashar left off!" the woman laughed.

"I never had a problem dating a Black man. I was more concerned about finding the right man, which to me, is more important than color."

"Black people are a trip too, girl! I see the way they break their fucking necks to cop a look at you when we're out shopping sometimes. How do you handle it?"

"I don't pay that bullshit any mind, Sam. I have a great husband. If I didn't, it might not be so easy, but he is fucking amazing, if I do say so myself," Cyn said.

"Your eyes are sparkle when you talk about him. If you're not careful, that drought of yours might be over sooner than you think."

"Don't bet on it!" Cyn reprimanded.

Nadia and Leylah, filled with mischief, knocked over the sandcastles the boys had spent the afternoon building, which led to tears for their mommies, and jeers for the older sisters who were properly scolded as they headed back to the house for a family dinner.

The sun-filled summer days at the house provided lots of bonding time for the women. Cyndarella checked on work remotely using her iPad and fielded a few phone calls as they came her way. Denise appeared to be enjoying working out on the West Coast, for it brightly showed through her work, and she was sure that more awards would be coming the agency's way. It made her proud knowing that her employees were recognized as she was for their efforts. It wasn't all about her; Peachtree was all about teamwork.

Chapter Thirty-One

T he family decided to hang out in the basement when
mid-morning showers interrupted their outdoor plans. Willa
drove Cyn nuts about Nadia's hair because she kept getting sand in it at
the beach. Black women didn't play about with their hair and water, as
it did not mix well; it didn't matter what grade of hair it was. Nadia was
now sporting two long braids, courtesy of Grandma Willa.

While the boys played on the PS3 gaming system, the women
played a mean game of Apples to Apples Junior edition with Leylah
and Nadia. The boisterous bouts of laughter almost drowned out the
sound of the doorbell upstairs. One of the local fisherman had dropped
off freshly-caught walleye and whitefish earlier this morning and they
weren't anticipating any other visitors or guests.

"Cyn, come with me to see who's at the door," Samira said.
Cyndarella was surprised to see Bashar, with Faisal and her brother,
Pete, in tow.

"Oh shit! You've got to be kidding me! What are you guys doing
here?" Cyn sulked, as the men laughed at her sarcastic candor.

"It's good to see you too, love!" Bashar snickered, as he gave his wife
a brief kiss and hug.

"Faisal, you couldn't wait two more days for us to come home?"
Samira asked in disgust. "Holy shit!"

"Hell no, I wasn't going to wait another day without seeing you,
and this one," he said pointing at his brother, "was going crazy over Cyn
and the kids. C'mon, honey, lighten up, already."

Pete had been warned on the trip up about the chaotic and
craziness of his sister and the in-laws. Bashar was like a little brother

to him when he'd dated his baby sister in high school, and now the marriage solidified their relationship even more so.

"Y'all can argue all day, but somebody tell me, where is my momma?" Pete asked.

"Let's go downstairs where everyone is in the games room until the rain stops," Samira said, as she led them down the basement, where the men received a better reception than they had when they arrived.

"Hey, Mom! What's up, Mrs. Bazzi?" Pete greeted each lady.

"How are you, baby? You left my poor husband home alone. Did he wear you out with all of those outside chores he had for you?" Willa inquired.

"Nah, Ma. It's been good for me being around Dad again," Pete replied, as he and the fellas joked with the children who were thrilled to have their dad and uncles around. Pete noticed his sister watching Bashar playing with their kids. For a moment, their eyes met, and she looked away. He felt the need to approach her, as they had become closer since he'd gotten a divorce. She was less judgmental of him, and that had opened the door for them to start the healing process.

"You can't keep avoiding that man, sis. He really loves you, girl. I don't know why! I tried to talk him out of it and told him he is out of his damn mind, but he won't listen" Pete joked.

"Peter Vernon Worthy, dearest brother. I'll let you in on a little secret. I'm partially letting him out of the doghouse, okay? The rest is truly going to be on him," Cyn admitted. "We just needed a little space, that's all."

"I'm not here to judge you either way. But it matters to me that you are happy. Bashar's the real deal. He's a good guy." Pete spoke as his brother-in-law sauntered over to join the conversation.

"Did I hear someone mention my name?" Bashar asked. Pete nodded his head.

"I'm leaving you with your wife."

Cyndarella saw Pete walk over to the rest of the family, leaving her with Bashar who carefully studied how relaxed she appeared. Cyndarella continued to dazzle at in her early forties. Her hair which normally would cascade down her back was pulled up into a ponytail, and her skin was glowing against the chic coral shorts romper she wore that had a deep V-neckline, and the taupe wedge heel sandals that accentuated her legs.

"Why are you staring at me so hard?"

"I've missed you. And our babies," he put forward. "I really have been thinking about us, about making it right again, but it's not fair for me to have to do it by myself," he professed. "I hate it when you tune out and shutdown."

"Bashar, just because you know me better than anyone, doesn't mean you can control my reactions. Sometimes, I wish you'd stop crowding me and just give me my damn space!" Pausing momentarily, she continued, "I missed you as well, love. You need to understand that the fit of fury you had raged out of control and was pretty unsettling for me. Am I making sense to you?"

"I completely comprehend what you're saying. I'll try not to crowd you."

"Thanks. That's a start."

"But, Cyndarella, you need to know when I heard you were trapped with Thad, I was uneasy, but maintained my cool. Then Faisal and I overheard all that garbage he was talking to you, and my post-traumatic stress syndrome kicked in. All I thought of was rescuing you and killing that son of a bitch!" he confessed. "I accept that, but can we to move forward, Cyn? It's been six weeks since you kicked me out of our bed. Six weeks! We've never gone five days without making love before this. We're leaving after lunch. I have something special planned for you," he added.

"Oh, please, I bet you still found time to relieve yourself by masturbating, my love," she teased. "Where are we going?"

"Don't worry about it. Go pack, as I spend time with the kids. Then, my dear, we're out of here," Bashar advised, while playfully swatting her on her bottom. Cyn walked away, but then came back and genuinely hugged her husband and shared a kiss. The elegant scent of patchouli and floral notes of the perfume she wore drew him in even more.

The adults in the room observed Cyndarella's icy façade towards Bashar soften, which tickled them. The women agreed to watch the children for Bashar, as they knew the couple needed some alone time. Willa excused herself to tend to Cyndarella as she packed.

"You need some help?" she asked her daughter.

"Not really. If I leave anything, take it back with you and I will get it from you later, alright?"

"You got it. So it looks like all is forgiven. Who knows, after this little break, Bashar might knock you up again," Willa snickered.

"Mom! Don't say that! I told you we are done!"

"When you get your tubes tied, or Bashar gets a vasectomy, I'll stop saying it!"

Cyndarella packed, while spending time with her mother who thanked her for the vacation.

"Are you going to be alright with me leaving?" Cyn apprehensively asked. She knew her mother was quite social and could fend for herself, but it was only right she made sure that Willa was fine.

"Who do you think your husband called to ask if it were okay for him to come up here to begin with? This extended family of yours, for the moment, is *my* family, as well."

Bashar and Cyndarella left the house without incident. Zaid, their youngest twin, didn't handle their departure as easily as she'd have liked him to, but they managed to calm him down. Cyn enjoyed the beautiful summer weather as they drove down I-94, even though she had no clue as to where they were headed.

Chapter Thirty-Two

Denise and Marla had spent the last month soaking up natural Vitamin D in the form of the sun out in Orange County. They stayed in Newport Beach which was located in one of the busiest business districts in the area and situated next to the Pacific Ocean. The Island Hotel's proximity to nearby beaches gave the duo time to enjoy waterskiing. They also hung out at Newport Back Bay where they rented bikes and rode along the trails. The biggest adventure for Denise's preteen was shopping at the upscale Fashion Island.

Neither of them was eager to go home, but Denise reminded Marla that she had to send her back to get ready for school. This was the first time in Marla's life that she had ever been separated from her father this long and it bothered her. Denise hadn't spent lots of time on the phone with Sean as she normally did, so sometimes for her daughter's sake, she'd pretend she was talking to him and it appeased her daughter.

Marla had spent two weeks at a Performance Arts camp in Anaheim, with the granddaughter of Gunnar, and they'd had a blast. It also gave Denise time to come to grips with the changes her body was undergoing with her pregnancy. She was fourteen weeks in now, although she hadn't begun showing yet. She'd gotten most of the work for the beverage account in alignment with the national campaign goals, and their presentations were executed unblemished.

Cyndarella was due to come out for some meetings, but with Denise in situ, the immediate need for her friend to be present was taken away. Denise blocked Cyn's attempts to come out several times, as she wasn't ready for her big reveal to the world. She needed time. As long as she was producing at the highest level possible, Cyndarella would stay put, or at least Denise hoped she could continue to persuade her friend that she had it all covered. That would only work so long as Cyn micro-managed her business dealings like a hawk.

Her attorney had a process server present Sean with divorce papers at home. Dee made sure he wasn't embarrassed at work. They would divide their joint assets, and she'd requested to keep the house. There was no time to pack up and move with a new baby, now. The important thing for her was to give him the freedom he appeared to need desperately so he could do whatever he pleased.

Marla had gone into her bedroom at the two-bedroom suite they shared at the Island Hotel, and turned in for the night when Denise received a text from Sean asking her to give him a call.

"What's up?" she drily asked.

"I'm coming out there so we can talk about this divorce. And to bring Marla home to help her get ready for school." The words terrified the expectant mother.

"Sean, there's nothing to discuss. Let the attorneys handle it, okay?"

"Denise, I know I made mistakes. We both have, but you file for a divorce and have me served while you're three thousand miles away? That's fucked up! I'll email you my travel itinerary when I get it."

Denise's legs wobbled and she managed to sit in a club chair in her room. She couldn't let him see her like this, right now; for all she knew, she might start to show at any minute.

"Sean, I'm sorry, but you shouldn't have been surprised. You told me to contact my attorney and I did. I will never stand in your way," she replied. "Also, Cyndarella will be here next week, and she will bring our daughter home, alright?"

"Did you tell her about my affair?" he asked.

"She knows nothing. I promised you I wouldn't say anything to anybody, at least for now."

"Are you seeing somebody?" he asked.

"Why would that be any business of yours?"

"You can't answer that?" he challenged.

"Sean, no, I'm not, and if I were, you should be the first to give me your blessing!" she spat. "And I meant it when I told you to make sure you keep that bitch out of my house while I'm gone, do you hear me?"

"I would never bring any woman into our home, so calm down and get some rest. You're hormones still haven't settled, hun? You told me you'd come off the Clomid. By the way, CVS called and said you needed a refill a couple of times, but I told them to cancel it."

"Of course, my hormones are causing me to act crazy after I ditched the Clomid. Being out here isn't helping either. I am still adjusting to the time change and am quite sleepy, so, if you don't mind, I need to say goodnight."

"Give Marla a hug for me. I love you, Denise."

"Right!" she said and hung up the phone.

Denise had become the queen of diversion. There were upcoming interviews Cyn needed to come out to California for, which would work in Denise's favor and get Sean off her back. He didn't sound like he wanted a divorce, but he hadn't said he didn't want one either.

Chapter Thirty-Three

Vette called Pete several times and his phone kept going to voicemail. She figured that he might not have a good signal up in South Haven. They had gone out for drinks a couple of times, and she'd really enjoyed their outings together as friends. Julia had surprised everyone when she came to the Worthys' garden party, including herself. She also remembered the dirty looks Julia gave her throughout the evening.

Pete was divorced, and if something developed between them, she'd dump Louis to be with Pete, without question. Men had too many excuses, including her current one. They longed to control the pace in relationships at a speed which benefitted their feelings most. She was sick of it!

The situation with Tavie and Orville had confused her about the whole marriage thing. Was it really worth it anymore? Or were she and Tavie stuck with the wrong guys? Apparently Tavie hadn't completely given up yet, for she was still keeping Orville at bay. Cyndarella and Bashar had been solid until Thad had reappeared and Bashar caught a case. Denise seemed distracted and was vague in the phone calls they managed to have, which really wasn't like her at all. She wondered if Denise had finally come to terms with the fact she couldn't get pregnant, and that Sean wasn't supporting her like he should. Who knew? She sure as heck didn't.

Louis was buried into a major corruption case for the city of Detroit. It left little time for him to spend with Vette and the children as he prepared for the rather lengthy trial. He looked over at Vette, as she sat reading the Detroit Free Press newspaper on his couch. After the trial was over, he would marry Corvette in a small ceremony. He wasn't opposed to making it a dream wedding for her, but on a smaller scale. The problem was, he was unsure of whether it was something she really wanted from him anymore. She picked up the sports section of the paper to find him studying her.

"Louis, what's wrong?" she asked.

"This case has gotten on my last nerve, that's all."

"You seem like you got a lot on your mind. Anything I can do to help?" she asked, as he laughed, getting up from the desk in his home office to join her on the couch.

"Corvette, this case will be over soon, and there will be some changes around here. You will be front and center, my love, but only if it's something you truly desire."

"Shit, Louis! Is that a proposal? Are you proposing to me?" she squealed, dropping the newspaper she had been reading.

"We can discuss the details later, if you're still up for it." Louis kissed her on the forehead, as she sat smiling at him. He hadn't seen her that happy in months, and he had a hunch that Pete Worthy, her best friend's brother, had something to do with it. He was good at reading people, and Pete seemed pretty taken with his lovely ex-wife. He wouldn't have thought much of it until the woman asked if him directly if he was with Vette. Louis had asked why, and she said that they looked pretty chummy to him. He'd looked over to where they were, and he'd had to admit, they did.

Louis, from the first day he'd met Vette, had known she was different and, in time, it became evident to him he'd found a keeper in the quirky woman, even though their road to happiness had some bumps in it along the way.

Chapter Thirty-Four

"The boy is mine. I didn't want to tell you this over the phone." A worn Orville spoke as he sat next to Tavie on the couch. "Tavie, baby, I'm so sorry!"

Orville had got rid of his trademark dreadlocks and got his hair cut short. He looked like a different man to her without them—sexier. The removal of the dreads no longer concealed the youthful look of the man before her. His dark skin seemed a replication of the mood he found himself in. If he stood next to a former cast member in *Grey's Anatomy*, the handsome Isaiah Washington, you'd think they were brothers.

There was nothing to prepare Tavie for how she'd responded. The emptiness she felt inside for being the so-called good girlfriend to a man who'd deceived her made her shed tears which she wiped away. He continued to give up more details that complicated the issue even more.

"Geneva is married. That's the one fact that she left out when she told you about Nathan. She married some wealthy financier from Bermuda, and she wants to spend time traveling with him around the world before Nathan starts school."

"In other words, dump the kid on you, right?"

"Exactly. I need you now, Tav. Please don't walk away from me. Us."

"You *need* me now?" she huffed. "You didn't need me when you were fucking her, did you? Before and after she had *your* son! I don't even know why you divorced her in the first place!"

"I only slept with her a couple of times after she had our son. She told me she'd broken up with child's father. The dude she's married to now would often be there when she invited me over to dinner with a group of mutual friends. We weren't alone a lot. It wasn't a long-term affair," he stressed, as beads of sweat formed on his forehead.

The news made Tavie lightheaded. She stood up and her heartbeat seemed to accelerate to the point she couldn't catch her breath. She rubbed the front of her neck, then tried breathing a deep breath through her nostrils and slowly exhaling as a calming mechanism, but it didn't help. Making her way over to the kitchen, she opened the refrigerator and grabbed a bottle of water. She looked out the kitchen window, as Orville stood behind her, giving her left shoulder a light rub.

Orville knew she was angry and the disconnect in the communication between them was profound. He wanted her bad. He began to kiss her neck, which she seemed to respond to, but then she turned to face him and shook her head to say no.

"Stop, alright? Just stop!" she said, hoping he would listen. As strong as she wanted to be at the moment, she needed him, though not all the nastiness that came with loving him. She walked to her front door and said it was time for him to leave.

"Okay. I'll leave, but we both know that's not what you want."

"For right now, it's best," she managed.

"Open the door for me, then," he requested, and she proceeded to do so. She reached up to turn the deadbolt lock, where upon Orville began to gently bite at the nape of her neck. His breathing was rapid and she could feel his heartbeat on her back as he pressed up against her. Slowly, Tavie turned around to face him and the two shared a steamy kiss in the foyer.

With her back pinned against the door, Orville removed his shorts, exposing his considerably-sized penis which she was well accustomed to. He leaned in and bit her hardened nipples through the cotton black lace cami-tank top she wore. He gathered her up and carried her to the bedroom, where his attention turned to her breasts, touching and caressing them, making her moan in delight.

He opened her legs and planted kisses down each of them, unhurried. He removed her panties with his teeth, and then tossed them to the side as she demanded he eat her. He tongued her wet hole until she was close to climax. She moved her pelvis nearer to his mouth, and held his head into place to release the orgasm that had built up inside her.

Tavie climbed on top of Orville's protruding dick and moved her hips, riding him hard until she felt the rigidity of his body and heard him groan out her name as his warm semen spurted inside of her pussy.

"What just happened here between us doesn't solve anything. It's going to take some time for me to know what to do."

"Tavie, you don't have to make a decision like this alone. We can do it together. I'll do anything you want," Orville said, as he sat up in bed. The thought of her ending their relationship made him uncomfortable. "Yeah mon, I fucked up, but I really do love you, girl."

"I know," she responded with a glum look on her face.

"I'm not cheating on you with anyone now. You can have my phone, check my messages; I've nothing more to hide from you. I want you to trust me again."

"Wow! That's big of you!" she quipped sarcastically.

"No matter what your decision is, I'll be okay. I just want you along for the ride. We are right together. I'm sure of it."

If only he'd been that sure when he was planting the seed of his offspring inside the womb of Geneva, then she could be sure. For now, everything was up in the air for them. But at present, she was going to take advantage of the time they were spending together today. After all, Orville just said he'd do anything she'd wanted. She'd make him literally eat those words.

Chapter Five

D r. Weiner paid attention to Mackenzie Dooley's manner as he spoke of his past relationship with Octavia. She was impressed by the gentleman's sense of awareness and accountability, and she took notes on them. He was an intellectual, not big on small talk. He dealt in facts. He was a fine-looking man with the appearance of a college professor, glasses and all.

"Dr. Dooley, if you openly cheated with other women while you were with Tavie, why did you bother being in any kind of relationship with her?"

"I didn't openly cheat in the sense that other women were knocking on the door of our home. It was implied, not blatant. She busted me a couple of times, but I wiggled my way out of it because I didn't want to lose her."

"Is that the pattern you have with most of the women you've been in relationships with?"

"Dr. Wiener, at some point in life, men will say anything to a woman for short-term gratification. Don't a damn thing else matter, other than being in that moment. I don't deny my wrong doing. I got counseling when Tavie and I broke up to work on myself."

"What did you learn from that?"

"Life is about choice. I was an arrogant, self-centered motherfucker sometimes and I happened to like myself more than the company I kept."

"Including Octavia?"

"I *loved* her, but got caught up in my own hype. I believed that no matter what, she'd always be right by my side. I told myself there was no way in hell Tavie would ever leave me."

"But she did," Dr. Weiner said, and he nodded his head in agreement.

"She did. And it sucked. We got back together on a trial basis, but then she got in over her head with Orville. End of story."

"How'd that make you feel?"

"Hurt and angry."

Dr. Weiner watched Mackenzie remove his glasses, which had begun to fog up with the moisture of tears, to wipe them. His feelings obviously were still raw, leaving him emotional.

"Can you elaborate why you were hurt and angry? You weren't innocent here, you know."

"I never said I was innocent. Dr. Wiener. Octavia and I were close to that happy ever after, but she didn't wish for it with us," he retorted. "She avoided me, changed school district, the works. Just saying the words, *It's over*, would have been better than what she did."

"Are you still in love with Octavia, Dr. Dooley?"

"I will always love that woman."

"And what about the current relationship you are in? What about this woman?"

"I care about Brenda. She's not complaining."

"What does she think about Octavia?"

Mack thought about how positive Brenda had been when he mentioned he was going to see Tavie's therapist. It blew him away.

"She's supportive. She said it may make our union better."

"That's commendable, Dr. Dooley. Have you seen or heard from Octavia since your dinner date?"

"She gave me your number to call. Other than that, I haven't, and I'm cool with that. I said I would come here. I did. I'm not trying to stir up anything with her, nor is she with me. She's in love with her fiancé," he deduced. "I'm not trying to meddle with that."

Dr. Weiner recognized the turmoil of the entwined connection of Mackenzie, Octavia and Orville. The dynamics of this relationship had shifted in a way that could end with disastrous results. The tensions of the past versus the present with all parties needed to be contained. Her hope was that she'd be able to steer her patient, Octavia, in the right direction and as logically possible.

"Fair enough, Dr. Dooley. I also think it is safe to say that you're keeping your distance because you don't want to get hurt again, correct?" the therapist questioned.

"Indeed."

Mackenzie agreed to come in for one more session with the therapist if needed. There was more to this story than she had anticipated. Mackenzie held high regard for his restraint to put himself out there with Octavia. It didn't seem to dawn on him that his former girlfriend might not have the same resistance to him that he appeared to have towards her.

Even though, as a therapist, it was a requirement she was supposed to be neutral, Dr. Weiner had to admit, the astute Superintendent of Southfield Public Schools had caught her off-guard as someone Octavia would have as a suitor, though it made sense why she would on the surface. One explanation that came to her mind was, perhaps, Octavia had fallen in love with the outer shell of the man, and not the inner man himself. That was what she needed to determine.

Chapter Thirty-Six

Bashar and Cyndarella drove up in front of the Amway Grand Plaza hotel, where a valet attendant and bellhop came to help them with their belongings. Holding hands, the couple walked into the lobby and noticed the elegant architectural details. Bashar led his wife over to the elevator. She was curious about where they were checking in. Bashar picked pressed the button for the twenty-ninth floor.

"Where are we going? We've just passed the check-in desk," Cyndarella asked as the elevator door opened up.

"A place where Security won't disturb us when you get all hot and bothered," he laughed.

"I can never live that down!" she said, as they reminisced about the time Security was called because they thought she was in danger. After failing to make themselves heard by knocking on their door, they repeatedly called the room to ask if everything was okay. Finally, Cyndarella picked up the phone and shouted loudly, "I'm in the middle of an orgasm!" and slammed the receiver down. Bashar tipped the manager $200 for his wife's outburst to smooth things over. They were lucky they didn't get thrown out!

Bashar guided her to an expansive suit with a 270 degree panoramic view of the Grand River and downtown Grand Rapids. The spacious luxury suite gave them instant access to pampering and gratification. Bashar had had the room filled with flowers, along with several presents located throughout the suite. Cyn was moved at the level of affection he'd shown her with his generosity.

"Nice suite," she said as she wandered throughout the spacious room. On the dresser there was an array of gift boxes on display for her.

She read the card and paused for a minute. "Bashar, thank you. You got to know that it's not about gifts for me."

"Consider it an early anniversary celebration. You know, it will be seven years next month."

"I know. God, it seems so much longer!"

They were interrupted by Cyndarella's work cell phone.

"Cyn, it's Dee. Have you checked your email? The beverage company's CEO would like to feature Peachtree in its online newsletter next month. They'd like to have you come out for a face to face meeting next week if you can. Gunnar will send his jet."

"I'm there. I'll send back my Outlook invitation later today."

"Great! I'll tell Gunnar as well. The team out here will be thrilled to know you're coming."

"Thanks, Denise. I will talk to you later."

"See you later, Cyn" Denise said as she hung up.

Bashar did not want to even think about Cyn taking off so soon after the lingering rift in their marriage.

"I know what you're thinking, and I have to be there. Why don't you fly out with me? You have a home there."

"Yeah, but my cousins are still renting it out. I could take care of some business out there. It might work."

"And you can take care of business *here*." She offered herself up, causing his tool to rise and expand in his pants. He knew his efforts had paid off, and he was further relieved that he and Cyndarella had a better understanding of each other's expectations. He needed to take action fast.

"Follow me." He led her to the marble-tiled bathroom that included a huge shower with a sitting bench inside. She quickly glanced at the sink where there was another present and he told her to go open it, which she did with widened eyes when she discovered what was inside. The black leather dom collar had stainless steel studs, formed in the shape of the letter B.

"This is lovely. Put it on me," she said, raising her ponytail while he placed it around her neck. "I thought we were making our own rules."

He turned on the water to the shower, and told her to get undressed.

"You don't get to make the rules anymore, at least not for the next forty-seven days. That's how long we've been playing by your set of rules. I will tell what to do and you'll do it."

"Got it."

"Get undressed and get into the shower."

She complied without hesitation. Cyndarella loved being his submissive and enjoyed going to great lengths in pleasing him, as he did her. Bashar joined her in the shower, where they took turns washing each other all over their bodies. He pulled the ponytail holder from her breast-length hair and it fell right at the side of her nipples.

"Where would you like me to begin," she asked.

"I want you on your hands in knees. Promptly!" he ordered, so she did it. "Damn, you bent over like this takes my breath away," he said, while massaging her ass. He reached for the leather whip and told her she was getting forty-seven lashings, one for everyday she'd withheld sex from him. "Let me know if it's uncomfortable for you and I promise to stop."

"I've been a selfish girl and I'm ready for my punishment. Spank my ass all forty-seven times. I can handle every single lick."

The leather whip crashed down on the tender cheeks of her round brown ass. The first series of hits didn't seem to bother her. It wasn't until the count of twenty that a loud groan escaped her mouth.

"Faster, harder!" she cried out, as he continued to spank her at a quicker pace. The beautiful sight of her brown ass popping up in his olive-skinned face nearly made him come undone, as she shivered in anticipation for the remaining five licks.

He rubbed his hands over her bottom as warm water from the shower sprayed on them. Cyn sat up for a moment, and he could tell by the look in her eyes she needed more. He led her to the ledge in the shower, where she propped one leg up on the bench and bent over for him to fuck her.

Bashar began to work himself inside her tight, juicy, willing pussy. He did so slowly, inserting a fraction of an inch at a time into her hole, then abruptly removing it. He did this methodically forty-seven times, sending her over the edge.

"More! I need more!" she begged, as she pushed back harder on his cock.

"You want more of this big beast, don't' you?"

"Oh, yes! Yes!" she groaned. He kissed her on the back and reached up to turn the faucet off. "Let's get out of here," he said, leading her to the giant king-size bed with plush bedding.

"Lay down on your stomach for me. I'll be right back," Bashar instructed, before he left the room to retrieve his wife's AHAVA Honeysuckle and Lavender body cream to massage into her dry skin. He didn't want his baby to turn ashy, something women of color were plagued with. He had dry skin but it didn't show up on him, or Nadia, but the boys had taken after their mother and their skin was just as dry as hers.

The silky texture of the lotion saturated his hands while he gently massaged her neck, back and shoulders with the cream that had an exotic, calming scent. Her sighs of pleasure made it harder for him to concentrate as he rubbed her plump ass. He could see raised welts from the spanking he'd given her.

Bashar knelt down behind Cyn, who was on all fours again, and ran his tongue between her pussy lips and clit. She was in a euphoric stupor while he ate her out. The sounds she made caused tensions of desire to build up in him again, as she moaned for him to fuck her. Cyn propped herself up on her forearms, arching her back, trembling as she climaxed. She was on fire as he crouched down and guided his long, slightly curved, erect manhood into her wet entrance.

The head of his cock throbbed as he began to position himself deep inside her. The tightness of her womanhood wrapped around his cock, snug enough to milk him like a cow, even before he had completely entered her. He wasn't anywhere near wanting to come.

"Oh God, Bashar! Your dick feels so good! Please, I need more. Make me come!"

"Not now. I've got forty-seven days of loving to make up for. I'm going to ride this sweet pussy for a while before I unload inside you."

"Ah, Ah, Ah!" she murmured repeatedly. The weight of his balls intermittently banged up against her highly-stimulated clit, bringing her closer to completion.

"I'm about to come."

"No," he said, and pulled out of her to switch positions. "Are you okay?"

"No. You know I can't ever get enough of you," she spoke softly. Without missing a beat, Bashar rolled his wife onto her back and positioned himself between her legs. Cyn's hand trembled as she helped guide his penis inside of her. Neither one of them could take their eyes off each other as each of them were consumed by their love for one another.

She held her legs up high in the air as he went to work on her pussy, with her juices spilling down on his cock.

"Ooh, ooh, yeah! Fuck me!" she squealed. Bashar's mouth claimed hers, drawing her into a passionate kiss. The lust in her eyes she had only for him made him devour her more. She couldn't have looked more desirable to him, even in her vulnerable, submissive state.

"That's it, baby, you like grinding on this big dick, don't you? Grind on me until you get enough."

"C'mon, give it to me, Daddy. Give it to me!" she insisted in a raspy voice.

"You're sure?"

"Absolutely!"

He plunged into her deeper like a bulldozer, as he yelled out to her, "Whose pussy is it?"

"It's your pussy! You can have it anytime you want!"

"Come with me, Cyn," he interjected. The buildup of his impending eruption allowed him to pump inside of her in a frenzy until he hosed her, drenching her hotbox with fluids of his love.

Chapter Thirty-Seven

Bashar and Cyndarella enjoyed an early dinner at Cygnus 27, atop the Amway Grand Plaza hotel. It had been awarded one of the few Four-Diamond restaurant marks of distinction in the state of Michigan. They sampled light appetizers of tuna ceviche and Chesapeake Bay oysters, and then enjoyed a bowl of seafood bisque in a private dining room. They ordered a vintage bottle of Dom Perignon to share over their meal.

Cyndarella felt blessed that they could enjoy a pricey meal without constantly worrying about cost. She'd had enough of that in her previous relationships. Peachtree was now generating over a million dollars in revenue, something she did not take for granted. Bashar's businesses generated more than hers. As a couple, they were still financially conservative and splurged only when they felt necessary.

"Cyn, I wanted to let you know I hired a private investigator to help Faisal and me piece together out what really happened to me back then in Iraq."

"I know you've struggled dealing with it. I hate you have to go through this shit," she replied, while rubbing his hands.

"It's a mystery, and with Father's death, I will never be able to get answers from him. Was it in retaliation against him in some way and I was used as some kind of pawn? Baby, I just don't know, but I am determined to find out."

"You need closure, and whatever you need from me, you've got it. I want to know as much as you do, so we can put this behind us."

The waitress asked if they were interested in the dessert menu, but both politely said no. They made their way back to their suite where more loving ensued.

Discarded clothes were thrown aside in the suite, as the temperature of desire rose inside of them. Cyndarella was kneeling in front of Bashar on her knees with her warm mouth around his dick, stroking him deep-throat style, taking him whole. He ran his fingers through her hair as she turned her face to the side and sucked upwards while locking eyes with him, looking like a perfect sexual goddess.

Bashar knew his wife gave him the ultimate gift most men never got from their partners. She had given him her body, mind and soul. The love she had for him was unguarded. He'd had relationships with women before they'd reconnected, yet they'd never measured up to her, on any level. There wasn't a doubt of the absolute submission she gave to him. There was a pureness in the fact she liked to perform all the kinky things that he liked. He aggressively thrust further into her mouth, at the same time as her tongue performed acrobatic tricks that caused him to wince in pleasure.

"You're so close, baby," she announced to him. "I can taste your pre-cum."

"Fuck, Cyndarella! That mouth of your is a bad motherfucker!" he declared, as his dick continued twitching in reaction to her suckling and moaning.

Bashar grabbed her head to remove it and led her over to the bed.

"I want some pussy. Come give me my pussy that you've been depriving me of," he said, as he lay down on his back in bed.

She had no problem doing what she was told. She climbed on top with her perky breasts and hardened nipples facing him. He greedily attacked her left nipple with his mouth, while squeezing her right nipple with his fingers, then alternating between the two.

Bashar was the love of her life, and she'd never, ever let him go. He belonged to her, and she him. It wasn't negotiable. They met pelvic to pubic bone; her hips moved up and down as he raised his pelvis to meet the ferocity of her movements with animalistic passion until they both came.

Chapter Thirty-Eight

"I want to go home when you go, Mom!" Marla whined. "Why can't I go home with you?"

"That's not possible, Marla. You need to get ready for school."

"But what about you, Mom? When are you coming home?"

"I need to be out here a few weeks more. I'll be home before school starts, so don't worry."

"What's going on with you and Dad?" the inquisitive preteen asked.

"What do you mean, what's going on between your father and me?" Denise replied.

"Forget it, Mom! I'm not stupid, you know! All you do is yell at him and he looks miserable. Besides, Dad would have come out here to visit us, I'm certain of it. Is it because you're too old to get pregnant?"

Denise was floored that she was having this conversation with a twelve-year-old who she and Sean were both trying to shield from their problems. She could see that they were not doing a great job.

"Your father did want to have another baby. The meds I took made me aggressive towards your father because of hormonal changes. It was nothing more than that."

"You're not going to get a divorce are you?" Marla interrogated. "I'm really afraid, Mom."

Denise hugged her daughter to assure her that their family would be alright, even though it wasn't the truth and she wasn't sure they would be. Marla was doing well in school and she didn't want her daughter to start acting out because of the impending divorce. She couldn't read Sean. He seemed remorseful, but resolute now on them dissolving the marriage.

Denise knew she'd have to level with Cyndarella, as her breasts and face were swollen, and, as of late, her belly had started to slightly protrude. She'd stopped off at a convenience store to pick up some tampons to throw Marla off the scent. All of these tricks made her exhausted.

Marla had her bags packed with all of her clothes, except for the outfit that she would be wearing when she went home. She felt like crap because her parents were still trying to have kids and she felt they were too old. She never stopped voicing her opinions to her parents.

"Who has babies in their forties, Mom?" she asked her mother. "That's old!"

"It is not! Goodness, child. Couples are waiting longer to get their careers in place in order to be able to afford a family."

"Whatever, Mom. You should've had one right after you had me, like Dad said, and there wouldn't be all of *this* fighting. You guys would still love each other," Marla sulked, and walked out of the room to turn in for the night.

Denise was in her second trimester, and her doctor had arranged for her to get a test to make sure there were no developmental issues at a local OB-GYN office in Newport Beach. The results were due any moment, and though they were preliminary, she could find out the sex of their baby if she opted to and she couldn't wait to find out. She felt remorseful not sharing this moment with Sean. The thought occurred to her that waiting to share this with him might repair their relationship, but she felt it was best she go it alone. After all, it was where she was headed.

Denise had a dilemma. While she'd been away, she'd really developed a liking for the West Coast. Her time there had produced the serenity of a tranquil vacation, even though she on business. The occasion allowed her to clear her head, and the burning question that dogged her now was should she tell Sean she was pregnant, or wait until she went home? Cyndarella also loomed largely in the scenario, for what if she chose not to keep Denise's secret once it had been told? There were no guarantees that she would do so, and it troubled Denise tremendously.

Chapter Thirty-Nine

"Uh-oh, Mom. Quick, come here!" Marla yelled out. "In the bathroom!" Denise went to see what the ruckus was about.

"Look," she said, holding her panties in her hands while she sat on the toilet. "I've got my period!"

Denise took the panties from her daughter to examine the evidence, which proved indeed that her daughter had begun menstruating. It bought tears to her eyes.

"Marla, how do you feel? Any cramps?" she asked.

"I'm mad! I messed up a favorite pair of my panties! And no cramps. Will it always be so unpredictable?"

"No, it won't. You should expect it every twenty-eight days. We'll mark the day on the calendar so you'll know when to expect it next."

"It might be irregular at first though, right? Like what we read in the health books."

"You're on it. We have to tell your father about this."

"Mom, it's embarrassing. You tell him!" she said.

"Take a shower, and I'll go downstairs to get you some mini-pads."

"Can't I just borrow one of your tampons?" Marla innocently asked.

"Not right now. We need you to get used to what your flow will be like, and then we'll switch you over to tampons, alright?"

"Fine, mom. I'll take my shower. Hurry up so I won't bleed to death!" she joked.

Marla had gotten her period for the first time which was an unforgettable moment, and Denise was glad that they were together when it happened. There were few options in the gift shop of the hotel. The box of twelve Always mini-pads cost $7.00. She paid cash for them instead of charging the item to her room. While she was waiting for the elevator in the lobby, Sean phoned.

"Hey there!" she said. "What's going on?"

"The Operations Manager got fired, and they're bringing someone in from Corporate to take over in the interim. Of course, we have an upcoming meeting next week with the newbie. It'll be interesting."

"Wow! That's radio for you. I have some news for you too."

"Aw, shit, what now?" he asked.

"Marla got her period today."

"Really? How'd she take it? Is she scared?"

Denise laughed as he ambushed her with questions.

"She's fine. I've actually just bought her some pads."

"Damn! I don't want to even think of my baby girl growing up so fast on us like this."

"She's embarrassed to tell you."

"She shouldn't be," he replied. "We always talked about doing something special for her when she got her period. I'll go out and do something for her, and surprise her when she gets home."

"That would be wonderful."

"Damn! I'll be the only man in the house with two hormonal women. God help me!" he kidded. "Well, at least for now".

"Stop your nonsense, Negro! Bye!"

"Hold up! Why you in such a rush? Are you on your period too? I feel like I'm on this long roller coaster ride that won't end. You've been quite testy and passive-aggressive, especially with the divorce papers, babe. What's going on with you?"

"First of all, I need to go back upstairs so Marla can have her pads. Secondly, you had an affair, remember? I know I do. And lastly, I'll reserve the rest of my answer for when I come home. I'll have Marla give you a call. Goodnight!"

"Bye," Sean glanced at his phone, and was tempted to call Denise back, but he'd wait to speak with his baby girl. He felt more protective of her than ever. Marla's young body had already started developing breasts, and she appeared older than she was. He'd already seen some men checking her out. He'd catch a case in a minute if some teenage boy tried to run up his daughter. Divorce or not, Sean was compelled to take care of his family.

Chapter Forty

Sean's affair with Ursula Collins had come to an abrupt halt. She took the news literally lying down, on her back. He'd told her he couldn't continue on with their sexual liaison anymore. He'd confessed everything to his wife, including Ursula's identity.

Ursula requested that he give her a farewell 'tune-up'. He obliged. The fifty-one-year-old woman worked out five days a week, and had the stamina Denise sometimes lacked. There wasn't an ounce of fat on her five-foot-nine-inch body. Her impressive physique had won her a bodybuilding championship for her age group. They'd met through a minority networking event a few years ago in passing. It wasn't until she started working out at his gym that they'd become reacquainted.

Sometime last year, in the middle of one of his workouts, Ursula had made a play for him. They were both married which took the pressure off him. He'd avoided getting involved with single women if possible because, for him, it was simply a fuck to let off some steam. Denise had completely morphed into this controlling, dictating woman, which caused them to butt heads.

Ursula's twat clenched his rod like a master. It was incredible. He could only hope Denise would be able to do the things Ursula could do when she was the same age. Ursula's husband had health problems and she told Sean that sometimes he had a difficult time getting and maintaining an erection. Her husband ended up using a vibrator on her. Sean and his seasoned mistress used each other for sexual gratification. But he'd cancel his gym membership, now they were over.

Marla would be home in a couple of days, courtesy of Cyndarella. Denise had promised not to tell their friends about his infidelity. Especially Cyndarella! But he knew that there was a chance that Denise would have spilled the beans. He owed it to Bashar to tell him before his wife did. Bashar without question was genuine. He wouldn't be pleased to hear about the mess Sean was in. He hoped his friend's perspective might be of use to him.

Chapter Forty-One

"**D**enise is going to be surprised when she sees all of us!" Vette exclaimed, while the ladies were sitting on a private plane en route to Orange County, California.

"I know! I can't wait to see her, either. I feel like it's been ages since we've spent time together," Tavie agreed.

Cyndarella had decided to invite the women to accompany her when she discovered Bashar had work to tend to back home.

"She will be *thrilled*! And we get to bring Marla home. This will be a good trip."

"Thanks for inviting us," Vette said. "I needed a break from my kids."

"Tell me about it. I'm being honest; I really needed to be around you all again. This summer has gone by so fast and we haven't seen much of each other," Tavie confessed.

"Well, you'll have to fend for yourselves for most of the afternoon and the better part of the evening before I return."

"Girl, I'm just glad that you invited us down, and we could get away," Vette replied.

The women were sitting on the chartered jet chowing down on egg-white spinach and feta omelets, English muffins and Mimosas. The morning had been a blur; in less than an hour they would be touching down at John Wayne Airport. The eight-seat luxury jet with oversized leather chairs was so comfortable, they all fell asleep.

Cyndarella walked into the affiliate office of Latitude in a black, sleeveless, pinstriped A-line knee-length dress and a black belt. She also sported a sterling silver wide bracelet on her right arm. Her hair had been pulled back to give her a polished appearance. Her Roberto Cavelli sunglasses were removed as she approached the front desk.

"You look beautiful, Cyndarella!" Gunner said greeted the exhausted woman.

"Hey, Gunner!" The two embraced. Gunner gave her the once-over with his piercing gray eyes. "The look: I take it you approve?" she laughed.

"Damn right, I do! How's the family?"

"We're maintaining. I'm blessed to have them, well, at least some of the time!" she wise-cracked. They shared a laugh as he guided her into his office. They were on track to have a record-setting year in revenue. Peachtree had generated thirty-one percent of new business development revenue for the company, more than the other affiliate offices throughout the country. There were twenty-four including Peachtree.

"There's still more work that needs to be done here, guys," she said, drumming her manicured fingers on the conference room's cherry wood table.

"The trends are consistently strong, Cyndarella. You might want to consider having a greater share and become a partner, instead of an affiliate."

"Whoa! That would be fantastic, Gunner. But you know, I need to be methodical about a major decision like this. Whenever you're ready to pursue it, send over the paperwork to my legal counsel and we'll see what we can work out."

"Consider it done. You know something, Cyn? Denise is the best. She actually likes being out here. If we do make a partnership, you're more than welcome to have her transfer her family out here, if she's up for it," he offered.

"I'd hate to lose her, but that isn't my call to make, Gunner. I'm pleased that you like her work. Where is she, by the way?"

"She'll be back after your interview. You can catch up with her then. We're having a welcome reception for you over at the hotel."

"Wonderful. Looking forward to it."

His assistant buzzed in to inform them that Reilly Redding from Sparkling Spritzers and Smoothies had arrived. The two-hour interview included a half-hour photo shoot capturing Cyndarella in several corporate poses. She took a quick break to let her husband know about her conversation with Gunner. He said that they would discuss it upon her return. Her man always had a plan. Nothing distracted him if it pertained to business. She had the same acumen, though he urged her to go at it harder. They were a partnership in business and marriage, and she wouldn't want to have it any other way.

Chapter Forty-Two

Y*ou can do this, Denise, don't worry.*
The words spun in her head as she made her way down to the Oasis Bar inside the hotel. Gunner had arranged for Marla to spend her evening with his grandchildren by the pool at his home. She would be dropped off at the office in the morning. Denise had spoken briefly to Cyndarella earlier and got out of the Welcome Reception to go for an ultrasound. She was having a boy.

"Hey, bitch, where you been?" she heard a familiar face speak, and spun around in the direction of the voice.

"Oh my God, guys, you're all here!" Denise yelled out. Tavie gasped and was about to say something, before Cyndarella blurted out what everyone was thinking.

"Denise? What the hell? You're pregnant! Why didn't you say anything?" The waiter approached the ladies before she could answer. They plopped down on the oversized leather chairs in the bar and immediately placed their drinks order.

"Yes, ladies, I am pregnant. I'm in my second trimester."

"Shit! Seriously, and we're finding this out now because?" Vette barked.

The waiter appeared with their drinks, and Vette told him to keep them coming every half hour. She knew they had a lengthy evening ahead of them. Denise almost seemed reserved and so unlike her usual self.

"Is the baby, alright? Is that why you waited to tell us?" Cyn asked. "You need to start talking, Dee. Like right now!"

Moments later, the women were astonished by Denise's declaration about Sean's affair and the unexpected pregnancy she was handling alone in silence. Her main concern was getting through the pregnancy safely, without any stress.

"Damn, this is such a shame!" Tavie said crisply. "I can't believe Sean would do this to you!"

"Did he tell you who the ho is?" Vette asked. "Do you know her?"

"I've seen her in passing at some industry events. Cyn, you might know her: Ursula Collins, the Associate Director of Urban Marketing and Communications over at Wayne State University," Dee said.

"She's like in her fifties or something, right? Her husband is a professor and she's a bodybuilder, if I recall," Cyn said. "What are you going to do?"

"I'm still figuring it out, but I can't stay out here forever. I need to go home."

"Yes, you do, girl! It's your home too, Dee! If anyone should be leaving, it's his Black ass! So sick of hearing about cheating, dishonest-ass, motherfuckers! It's too close to what I'm going through, y'all," Tavie vented.

"Tell me about it! I'm starting to wonder if marriage is even worth it at this point in my life, on the real. Who can you trust? I mean I never thought Sean could be capable of some mess like this," Vette said.

Cyndarella took a sip of her Long Island Iced Tea, but it was clear from looking at her, that with her hand placed on her forehead she was in deep thought.

"Here's the deal. Every woman needs to be on bitch alert if they have an ounce of a good man, when he leaves the house, okay? These chicks nowadays will come at your man behind your back and in your face. Most of these sluts have low self-esteem and think there only worth is their vagina. They don't give a fuck about you. It's a game to them."

The women nodded their heads in mutual agreement. "Girl don't stop now. Preach!" Denise said, and Cyndarella continued on as the liquor bolstered her philosophical views.

"I'm not preaching, damn it, I'm teaching! Men are on dick alert too, but they don't have to be watchful as women. See, men tend to be more respectful when they see you out with your man. They might offer up a compliment if they get busted for checking you out too hard! Even as females when we're alone, most men will tone it down when they know you don't have interest. They loathe rejection, but the women welcome it the drama."

"Cyn, you should have been a psychologist. Every damn thing you just said is true. Ratchet hoes!" Tavie said. "Now you got me thinking of that skank, Geneva. I met Orville's son, Nathan. He's cute and all, but I can't do it. Every time I look at that boy, I'll think of how he got here and that I'm not willing to put up with it. Especially after this! I told Orville it's over!"

"Well," Denise said, after taking a swig from her bottled water, "stay away from Orville for good this time. You need to really mean it or you'll be knocked up yourself, and he'll be out like a ghost."

"Ursula is definitely not a twenty-something that Sean could knock up. She doesn't look her age, though the bitch couldn't take a compliment without bragging about herself. She's tall, muscular and thin. Complete opposite of me, whether I'm pregnant or not," Denise said with pity. "Sean thinks I've become too controlling. He's been pissed off because I did delay this, though I promised not to. I understand he was hurt. But did he have to hurt me too?"

"There are no winners here, Denise. You have to tell Sean about the baby. You're running out of time. This is what you're going to do," Cyn directed. "You're going to pick up that phone before the end of this week and tell him you're pregnant, and that you weren't sure if the baby would be viable or not, and you waited to tell him when you found out everything was going to be okay."

"Cyndarella! *Really*? What if he is still fucking that Mrs. Senior Citizen, bodybuilder trick?" Vette questioned. "She'll take his ass for all he's worth in court. Dee, you've got to change your approach to dealing with Sean at this stage with the whole control thing. Let it go for your sanity's sake. Take it from me, you need to do it with quickness."

Chapter Forty-Three

Vette frowned, wrinkling her nose in disdain. Her heart went out to Denise and she wanted to comfort her. "I agree with Cyn. You've got to get home, or this can get messier than it already is, Denise."

"Agreed," Tavie said, clinking glasses in a toast with the women. "So, I've been meaning to tell you guys that I had dinner with Mack. Geneva told him she spilled the news about Orville being her son's daddy, and he asked me out for dinner, checking in to see how I was."

"Oh, shit! You got to break the pattern of losers, Tavie! Seriously, look at what we're both going through! Though I don't think Sean is a total loser. I had a part in this, whether I want to admit it."

"He's not into me at all anymore. He went on to get his PhD and has a steady girlfriend, so good for him."

"Bashar met them out on the golf course a couple of times. I had dinner with them once, when I met Bashar at the clubhouse for dinner. I told you about it. They seemed pretty tight," Cyn chimed in. "Actually, Brenda invited us to some wine tasting soiree at her house, but we politely declined. That would have been a conflict of interest."

"Aw! That's my Cyn, loyal to the end!" Tavie chirped. "Mack did go to see my therapist on my behalf to let her know why I'm so fucked up."

Denise rolled her eyes. "Why in the hell would he do that?"

"Mack wants to help me, I guess. I am curious about what he told my therapist. I'll find out next week."

Vette looked at the other women seated at the table, and judging from her expression, she was less than thrilled to hear this. "Why can't you just ask him?"

"He hasn't called or texted me since I saw him, except to say he had a scheduled appointment with Dr. Wiener."

"You put up with a lot of shit from Mack, more than most of us would. Though, I did notice some changes in him towards the end, you know? You were flirting with the idea of getting back together. I honestly thought the way you were hugged up at my wedding, that the two of you would have been next," Cyndarella rationalized.

A tipsy Vette shouted out, "I'll second that! You had every right to be justifiably mad at Mackenzie. But he went to counseling for months by himself to get you back. It was that Jamaican jerk sausage that had you gone!"

Denise joined in, "You a fool, Corvette! Both you and Cyndarella are right, though. We were all surprised when you started taking up with Orville, Tavie. He's crazy cool, but we thought you and Mack would have that happy ending."

Tavie's eyes began to brim with tears. "My sense of discernment is apparently non-existent. Mack pleaded with me that he was ready to commit to me. I just wanted to punish him for using up all my good years."

"Hold up here. Uh, Octavia, you gave those years away for free. Don't put that all on Mack. He was there because you allowed him to be," Cyn snapped. "You're accountable, just like he was."

Vette shifted the conversation to her love life. "Louis is about to pop the question!" she grinned with a wide smile. "He all but told me so. I can't wait!"

"We can't either," the ladies said in a chorus.

"Bitches, I need to turn in for the night so my son and I can get some sleep," Denise announced. They shouted with glee, as she laughed at them. "I found out today."

"Whatever you do, don't name him Junior!" Tavie quipped, causing everyone to giggle.

"But before I go up, Cyn, everything alright in the Bazzi household after Bashar went cold Rambo on Thad?" Denise chuckled.

"We're good. And you will be too!"

"Bashar is the only man I think who won't cheat," Tavie said.

"I know!" Vette agreed.

"Don't be giving me the evil-eye, now. He is man, and as much he loves me, I cannot predict what he will or won't do. Though I told him he can cheat if he wants to and then I'll divorce him so fast and get with one of his cousins! He hates it when I talk like that!" she mused. "I wouldn't trade him for anything, that's for sure."

"And we know damn well, he wouldn't trade you with his fine ass!" Denise cracked up. "I don't know who's more sprung, you or him?"

"That's why she's knocked up all the time. They can't keep their hands off each other. They're both gone, y'all," Vette laughed. "Goodnight, Denise."

Denise gave the women hugs and they agreed to meet for breakfast in the morning. It was already past one o'clock, and she knew with the time change, they might stand her up. It was so good to be with her friends again. Their sisterhood fed her spirit, healing her inner turmoil, and made her whole.

Chapter Forty-Four

Tavie, Vette and Cyndarella remained down in the lounge for a quick cup of coffee before ending the night. They had to be present for Denise, and they had to keep quiet on the flight home with Marla in tow. Sean was supposed to pick his daughter up from Cyndarella's house, and Tavie and Vette wouldn't be staying tomorrow after they got to the Bazzis'. They didn't want to be near Sean, someone who they once held respect for.

"Do you think Bashar knows anything about this, Cyn?" a curious Vette asked.

"He will by the time we get home. He'll straighten Sean out, but won't get involved in their drama."

"Vette and I won't come in tomorrow when I pick up my car. Don't want to see Sean and show out in front of little Marla," Tavie surmised. "I'm still tripping on that bitch alert, dick alert thing, Cyn."

"Girl, you know Cyn's has a way with words. Her wordplay is fierce!" Vette boasted. "And so is your brother, Pete, girl!"

"What are you talking about?"

"I think Pete got to Lou. Seeing me with someone younger, having a good time at the garden party, made him wise up. I could tell he and Julia were jealous, which suits me fine. I'll get what I want one way or another!"

"I hope it's not my brother. He's a wildcard," Cyn alleged.

"I'm constantly praying for us. I never knew finding a soulmate would be so laborious," Tavie whimpered.

Between sips of coffee and continuous cackling, the night had come to a close, and they made their way to their rooms.

Chapter Forty-Five

Bashar listened intently to the bombshell that was being dropped as his childhood friend confided in him. He was so caught up into the world he'd created with his wife, it hadn't dawned on him that his old pal wasn't feeling the same way about his family. He refilled their sifters with another round of cognac.

"Man, Sean. Clearly you're going through some sort of mid-life crisis. I hear what you're saying, but my question to you is, why?"

"My ego is part of it, and trust. Dee and I mapped out everything before we got married, down to the number of children we were going to have and when we were going to have them." Sean spoke with contempt. "Trust is so important, man, and she broke it."

"I'm not completely following you, here. How did Denise break the trust in your marriage? Is she cheating too?" Bashar quizzed.

"She wanted to get our careers in place. Did that. Then she wanted to wait until Cyndarella got married. Just stupid shit with no real reason, other than she just didn't want to have another one until she was ready," he huffed. "As far as her cheating, haven't caught her doing anything, but I wouldn't put it past her."

"Damn! You're killing me, man! That's fucked up! I know you were pissed about the whole infertility thing you were going through."

"For sure. Bashar, Dee agreed with me, saying she wanted the same things I did, including a family. Then, what does she do? Put it off by making flimsy-assed excuses, and now she's hurt because it isn't as easy as it was the first time around for us."

Bashar was clearly affected by Sean's declaration. He knew his wife would be too. He paid attention as Sean talked about his mistress, Ursula.

"You hit a rough patch, dog. What did this Ursula give to you that Denise couldn't?"

"She kept things light. Nothing heavy. I've had a little flingy-fling here or there, but it was just the thrill of it."

"What in the fuck does that mean?"

"I never hit more than twice, if that. But then, I stopped doing that for about eight years, and then I started hooking up with Ursula."

"Why?"

"It was really innocent in the beginning. Ursula ran into me at the gym and we started working out together. I couldn't believe her body, man! At fifty-one, she could pass for a forty-year- old," Sean amused. "It was just drinks to begin with, and then she asked if I wanted to hit it and we started boning."

A lump formed in the back of Bashar's throat. He didn't know where Sean's head was, and he didn't appear contrite to him. Therefore, he began to dig more.

"So, where are you going with all this, Sean? So what if she has a good body! So does Dee! And this woman has a husband too!" Bashar roared, while he further questioned his friend. "Do you still love your wife, or what?"

"I love Denise very much, man. But we married young, right out of college. We were solid for years, but when that trust is broken, something inside you breaks too. I did, and can admit that. Maybe we might try therapy with our pastor," Sean offered.

"Sean, you and Denise need to counsel with each other before you go in front of anybody. You're both broken. Your marriage won't work unless you are willing to put everything out on the table. That's all I'm saying."

"Right, I'm with you, my friend, one hundred per cent. I feel like I married two different women. The more I gave in to her, the more she took without doing the same in return. She's selfish and controlling, and I'm not a fan of it one bit!"

The men continued talking in the kitchen, waiting for the women's flight to come in, and trying to bring order to the chaos in Denise and Sean's marriage.

"Bashar, you are lucky. Cyndarella is down for you all the way, submissive and all. That's special. I know somewhere up in this motherfucker you got a spare room just to store those chandeliers you got her ass swinging from!" Sean laughed. "But seriously, do you think that had you guys gotten married earlier, like we did, you'd still be this happy?"

"Hell yeah, my brother! I dated women from all over the world and partied like a motherfucker, but it was starting to get old. It was time to give up the game and settle down without having buyer's remorse. Cyn's my girl. She's not an easy woman to learn, but I was the man who could translate *her* language, *her* heart. All of that! Till the end, my friend, forever to the end."

"Wow, BB, that's some profound shit! I feel reenergized and ready to commit to Denise again. I ordered a lot of gym equipment for the house, so we can both work out together. I'm done messing around. We'll be stronger when the dust settles."

"You better mean what the fuck you say! I ain't claiming but one woman, and that's Cyndarella Echo Bazzi! I don't give a fuck about who claims anybody else. I ain't messing with those bitches out there. I know *my* woman!" he bellowed with laughter. "I still look when I see an attractive woman, but that's it."

"But what about the brothers trying holla at Cyndarella?" Sean couldn't help joke.

"Man, you don't want me to even go there! I'm down for honoring my wife, and if it were you with me instead of Faisal, you'd better have my back too!" The men laughed.

"You're an inspiration, Mr. Bashar Bazzi. Thank you for not judging me and hearing me out. I really needed to get this off my chest."

"What you *need* is to keep your dick in your pants, unless duty calls with the missus. Reconnect the right way; your family doesn't need to have it any other way. Especially Marla."

Mouna and Wiyad came by to drop the children off and visit with the men. Mouna went straight to the refrigerator and started cooking shish kafta with rice, while Wiyad made a fattoush salad for Cyndarella. Bashar said he wanted to order pizza, but he was overruled by his mother.

"Who gives their wife something out of a box after a business trip?" she'd chided, and Sean and Bashar got a chuckle out of that. They played with the children outside in the backyard, until Bashar got his wife's text to say that the ladies were on their way home.

Chapter Forty-Six

Marla was teary-eyed at leaving her mother. But she perked back up on the plane, pummeling her traveling companions with a barrage of questions.

"Did Mom tell you all, I…I got my period?" she asked in a hushed tone.

"Marla, that's wonderful!" Vette said, giving the young woman in waiting a hug.

"Ms. Vette, why is it so wonderful? I think it's gross! I'm walking around with blood coming out of me! I soiled a pair of my favorite white panties!" Marla cried out. "They were new!"

"I see your point. We've all felt the same way. It is pretty disgusting, but you somehow get used to it, and it's not so bad," Vette replied.

"Ms. Cyn, is it fun making babies?" Marla asked, causing the women to gasp and drop their jaws in shock. "I mean, my parents don't seem to be having fun. I know something about reproduction. It's *so* terrifying!"

"Marla, dear, it is terrifying, and making a baby is more a duty that is performed when a woman ovulating. It's not fun, it's work. Does that help you?"

"I understand a little bit. Is it painful when you ovulate? Or is it easier to perform the duty? Oh, I feel like I'm going to throw up!" she said clutching her stomach.

Tavie was aghast and in awe at this amazing girl growing up in front of their very eyes. How ironic was it for Marla to turn to them to ask them these questions, when little did she know that her own mother was in her current delicate state and would be much better equipped to answer her inquisitive daughter.

"Marla," Cyn forged on, "with any kind of work, you have to put forth effort and it can be more exhausting than painful. I'm afraid I can't answer any more questions for you. I know Denise would love to be able to make it simple for you to understand."

"Okay, Ms. Cyn. Thank you. I just thought the reason why you have more babies is because you and husband make it seem like it is fun, and my folks don't."

"Marla, would you like to play some games on my iPad?" Tavie asked to distract her.

"Yes!"

Tavie gave her the iPad, along with headphones, and Marla went to sit at the table on the cabin, and left the women totally floored.

"See, Cyn, even a kid can see how freaky you and your husband are!" Tavie doubled over in laughter at her friend.

"She wore your ass down. Shit, I'm over here still sweating!" Vette said, while she and Tavie made Cyndarella suffer with all their ribbing.

"Marla's something, alright. But look what she said about her parents. They don't seem to be having fun."

"It's sad. I wonder just how bad it is for them at home," Tavie wondered.

"Coming from the mouth of their daughter, it's not good," Cyn commented.

The flight home was a success and without incident. Each had their own personal agendas that needed tending to. Vette couldn't wait to see Louis. She'd pick her children up tomorrow, as they were at her sister's home in Milford where she lived on a horse farm. Both of her kids wanted to train to be equestrians.

Tavie had an upcoming appointment with her therapist, and felt disappointed she hadn't heard from Mack. Somehow all of this confusion with Orville was also propelling complete closure to the relationship she once shared with Mackenzie, and the impact of both losses was hitting her harder than she could have known. Dr. Wiener would need to help her make sense of it so she could move on.

"Look. My dad's here! There's his truck," Marla shouted. "Let's go in and you can say hello to him!"

"Marla, Vette and I have to get on the road, but we enjoyed you."

"Oh, please! Ms. Cyn, tell them to just stick their heads in and say hello. It's so rude not to!"

"Marla, go in and greet your dad. The ladies are tired and won't join us this time. I'll bring in your bag," Cyn spoke firmly. Her body tensed in apprehension of having to face Sean.

"Thanks, girl, for everything," Tavie said. "I really needed this trip!"

"Me, too," Vette said, as the women hugged each other goodbye.

Chapter Forty-Seven

Cyndarella smoothed out her light gray slacks, matching gray cotton body and silk infinity turquoise and silver scarf before she walked into the house, where the smell of fresh food greeted her growling stomach.

"*Marhaba, habibti*," Bashar greeted his wife in Arabic, the phrase meaning, "Hello, my love".

"*Marhaba, habibi*," she responded back to him, using the masculine tense, as they locked into an extended kiss and embrace. "Hello, everybody!" She greeted the rest of her family, and Sean.

Mouna grabbed Cyndarella's cheeks and gave them a quick pinch as a term of endearment. "How'd trip go, good?" she asked.

"Good," Cyn replied. "Sean, your daughter talked our ears off. She's amazing! I left her suitcase near the door."

"Thank you for bringing her home. She looks great. Two weeks is the longest I've gone before without seeing my girl."

"Mommy!" The cries of Cyn's brood rang out as they scurried over to her and she swooped down to give out hugs.

"Pick me up," Zaid dressed in a Sesame Street themed two-piece yellow short set demanded, as he outstretched his arms for his mother.

"How's my little munchkin?" she asked him.

"Daddy's teaching us how to potty," he said, throwing his arms around his mother's neck.

"Don't like potty!" Zahir spat out.

The gregarious twins with their cappuccino skin tone clamored for their mother's attention as she divided it among all three of her children.

"You're such babies!" Nadia snapped.

Cyndarella calmed the craziness down by passing out the souvenirs she'd gotten for the kids. Mouna and Wiyad had set the table for dinner.

"Come, it's time to eat!" Mouna called out.

"Can we stay for dinner, too, Ms. Cyn? Daddy?" Marla begged.

"You sure can," Bashar offered. "Go and grab a seat."

"You're sure, man? I don't want to impose on your family?" Sean said. He could sense the tension popping off from Cyndarella.

"You heard my husband, let's eat!" she said.

Chapter Forty-Eight

Vette was surprised to see Tara's car parked in Louis' driveway, and she wondered what her cantankerous mother was doing there. She was pissed because the car had blocked the access to the garage. She hoped her mother was okay; why else would she be home with her man?

Retrieving her bag from the trunk, Vette didn't notice Louis approaching her.

"Hey golden girl," he said. "How was your trip?" he asked, giving her a single red-stemmed rose.

"Thank you, Lou! My trip was fantastic! But I missed you, babe," she said as they shared a kiss. "We have company. Why is my mother here?"

"Why don't we go in and find out, shall we?"

Louis led the way to the house, and inside it was decorated with red and white flowers and heart-shaped balloons. A bottle of champagne was chilling in an ice-bucket placed next to glass flutes and where her mother, dressed in her nursing scrubs, sat wiping her eyes. Vette's heart began to pound as she began to tremble while Louis took her by the hand.

"Corvette, I've asked Tara to be here today because I want her to know how much I love you, and I am ready to spend my life with you. That is, if you're ready to be my wife?" he asked, then pulled out a De Beers two-carat yellow diamond solitaire ring set in platinum and yellow gold.

"Are you kidding? Yes, hell yeah!" she cried. "What about the trial you're so tied up in?" Louis placed the ring on her finger and it fit perfectly. "I *love* this! This is the ring I wanted. How did you know?"

"I told him everything. We looked at your Pinterest page," Tara said. "Louis, thank you for doing this while I'm still alive and have my wits about me. It took a black man to walk my baby down the aisle!"

"It's my pleasure," Louis said with a hearty laugh. "Let's have some champagne.

Corvette sent Tavie, Cyndarella and Denise a quick text to share the good news. She was concerned about Tavie for a moment, but she knew that her friend would be pleased for her.

"About my trial: I'm still entrenched in the shenanigans of it, but we can go ahead and plan a wedding."

"Are you going to have my daughter sign a pre-nup?" Tara solicited.

"Louis, don't answer that! Mother, stop it!"

"He has to! He's got his adult children's interests that he has to look out for. Don't lose sight of that, Corvette."

"Who wants another round of champagne?" Louis asked, changing the course of the exchange.

"I want to get married in December with red and white poinsettias all through the church. How does that sound?"

"Splendid, darling. Splendid!" Louis consented.

Chapter Forty-Nine

"How have you been holding up since your last visit, Octavia?" the therapist with the square-framed eyeglasses asked her.

"Well, under the circumstances. I spent some time with Orville and I even met his son. But I can't do it," Tavie announced.

"Is it because of the child that you believe you can't be with Orville?"

"My heart sank when I met little Nathan. I'd always resent him and that's not fair to either party. I honestly wish things could be different for us, but I cannot deny how I truly feel."

"Do you think it's possible that if you gave it some time, maybe your feelings might change towards Nathan? The reason I ask is because this is new for both you and Orville. It's not like he has a real bond with the child."

"Orville said the same thing. He really thinks we can make it work. I'm too daunted by the task to even try."

Dr. Wiener jotted observation notes while Tavie continued with her session.

"Dr. Wiener, what did you think of Mackenzie? Did he share anything of use that could help me moving forward?"

"I was wondering how long it would take before you'd mentioned him. Dr. Dooley provided me with background on your relationship that was helpful."

"I'm glad he did. I feel like I was in this bizarre love triangle, and for the first time in years, I am really just now mourning the loss of my relationship with Mack. It's weird to me."

"Why do you think that is?"

"Hmm. I was really angry, and didn't trust either of the men in my life. Orville was like this bad boy type that I've never been attracted to in my life. He also had an open marriage with Geneva, whom Mack had also been sleeping with."

"So you were trying to punish Mackenzie and Geneva?"

"Bingo! It was all about the revenge. *Sexual* revenge, to be specific," Tavie emphasized.

"I believe you've made your point. Though, now the tables have turned and you've really ended up where you started. Correct?"

"Of course, and it pisses me off! Orville leaves messages for me daily. Mackenzie, on the other hand, well, I really haven't communicated since I saw him last, and I wonder what he's been up to. You know, what's he thinking?"

The therapist knew Octavia's curiosity for Mackenzie's absence was drawing her closer to him. She didn't feel that this attachment was the healthiest for her patient, seeing that she had just called off her engagement.

"Do you feel you have closure with Mackenzie?"

"No. I don't have closure. Perhaps I never will. I didn't leave him on the best of terms. My friends just told me last week that they thought I'd made a mistake letting Mack go."

"What do you think?"

"Unfortunately, what I think doesn't matter much now. Mackenzie, you see, he's moved on with a really bright lady, from what I hear. I'm happy for him."

"That's courageous for you to be so accepting of everything."

"It's not like I have a choice. I'm okay with me right now. I need this time to clear my head, and I wish him the best."

Dr. Wiener noted Octavia had made progress. She was trending in the right direction, from all appearances. Mackenzie had closure, but undoubtedly Octavia hadn't. If the two kept a safe distance from one another, there would be nothing but smooth sailing ahead for them as they lived their lives separately. However, on occasion, life threw curveballs and turbulence, in that neither party might have enough time to run for cover.

Chapter Fifty

"Take it down, arch your back, slowly bring your booty in and come up and touch your body like you're putting on lotion," the dance teacher instructed Cyndarella.

"Itsy, I'm going to hate your ass in the morning. You're like a drill sergeant today!"

"Hey, I'm only doing what you're paying me for. We got to get you ready for your anniversary."

"Yeah, like in three weeks. Shit! Bashar is going to love it if I can ever get it down!"

"You could do it today if you had to. As long as you've been coming in to the studio, you're not that far off from your goal. Enough talking! Let's take it from the top."

Cyndarella left her dance class a sweaty mess. Her seventh anniversary was right around the corner and she wanted to do something memorable for her husband. He loved to see her dance, so she decided that she would have a couple of choreographed dances she'd perform just for him. She was also going to make him a DVD at the dance studio as a keepsake.

Thinking outside of the box was something that Cyn did in the blink of an eye. She always delighted him in some odd way or another, just to get a laugh out of him. She loved that he appreciated her zaniness, because she could be quite spirited at times. Love was in the air for her, and now for Louis and Vette, who wasn't kidding about her being a bridesmaid. She'd seen that one coming, so it wasn't a complete shocker. Denise and Sean's marital state was.

Cyn stopped off at Willa's house to pick up Nadia to take her for her first mani-pedi that afternoon. She reached inside her purse to grab a bottle of Neutrogena sunscreen spray to reapply to her daughter's apricot-colored complexion.

"I hope you don't create a monster with her doing this! You should wait a couple more years—she is not even ten!"

"Mom, I know that. She begged me and I promised I would. If she likes it, I'm sure we'll start doing it at home."

"Ooh, Cyn, I don't see how you like strangers touching you on your hands, when you get those massages," Willa said with chagrin. "That stuff's just not for me."

"I know, Mom. I know. I hear what you're saying. Today, it's just a mani-pedi, no massage."

"Can I have a massage?" Nadia inquired.

"Absolutely not! Let's go!" Cyn said to her daughter. She could only imagine how Bashar would respond.

"Bye, Granny!" Nadia rang out as they walked to the waiting vehicle.

Chapter Fifty-One

Denise wrestled with how to tell Sean she was pregnant. They'd had some really good discussions that were rather lengthy. She'd even fallen asleep while on the phone to him. They agreed they both wanted their marriage and not a divorce, and had areas of personal weakness they needed to work on.

Control was something she had to let go of and trust Sean completely. He was a freaking taskmaster and got the job done at work and at home—she'd loved that about him. A lot! The one area he couldn't delegate was when they would have a baby; she wouldn't give him any leeway with that. He hated to see her take birth control pills, but he'd picked them up from the pharmacy for her when she'd needed him to.

Sean told her he couldn't wait to see her on Friday, which got her thinking. She sent him a text and asked him if he wanted to talk via Skype, and he concurred. She was visibly showing now and that would be her big reveal, in addition to reciting the script of what Cyndarella had told her to say.

Denise logged onto her Skype account and greeted her husband while sitting at her desk.

"Hey freckles, what you been up to?" he asked.

"Finishing up here, and getting ready to come home."

Sean noticed the fullness of his wife's breasts and it turned him on. They looked like medium-size round oranges, making him want a little snack.

"Damn, Dee. Are you wearing a new pushup bra or something to try to keep up with them California girls? Your tits are huge!"

"They're supposed to be huge." She stood and proclaimed she was pregnant, showing off her swollen belly.

She continued to tell him that she waited to tell him until after she was given the green light that their baby would be okay. An emotional Sean placed his hands over his mouth, closed his eyes and took a breath.

"Wow! We're having another baby! I wish I would've known so I could've been there for you like you needed. When are you due?"

"Late March."

"We've got work to do. I say we put our place on the market and get a bigger house for our family."

"Okay. Sean, you need to slow down a minute. Are you truly alright with us keeping this baby and raising it together, and all? I mean, it's not the best time for us. You know what I mean?"

Before responding, he took in her words, while studying the worried lines of anxiety present in her face and felt guilty for the part he played to cause it. "Denise, I love you, okay? You've got to stop this neurotic bullshit. Our baby is coming into this world with two parents and a big sister who will love him or her, whichever it is.

"It's a boy, Sean. I'm carrying your son."

"Really? You had an ultrasound?"

"No. I needed to have one of those tests to make sure the baby didn't have abnormalities. The sex of the baby was optional. We get to see our son next week."

"Is it one of those 4-D ultrasounds that you can really see what they look like?"

"Yes, it is. I can't wait to see him!"

"Come home, Denise."

"I will be there in two days."

"I'll pay for you to come home tomorrow. *Please* do this for me. *Us.* Alright?" he pleaded.

"Fine. I'll let you take control," she giggled. "I'm coming home."

Chapter Fifty-Two

"Are you sure you don't want to buy my gown?" Tavie asked her friend.

"I'm sure," Vette said. "Thanks for asking".

"Alright then. I think I'm going to take it back to the bridal salon to exchange it for something else. I just don't want to hang onto something I may or may not wear. Is that wrong?" Tavie asked.

"That is so kind of you to offer something so special up for me! What's the hurry with you trying to get rid of it?"

"Maybe I'm a little superstitious. I'm afraid that if I keep it, I will never use it. I'm having a mental moment, I suppose."

"Stop beating yourself up. You've been through something really distressing. You're handling it a lot better than I'd be, that's for sure."

"I want you and Louis to have the best wedding ever. I mean that," Tavie said in a heartfelt way.

"I know, right? My man Lou came through. Damn, he had my heart racing in anticipation," Vette laughed.

"I know *that* feeling!"

"You will again in time, Tavie. Time is the biggest obstacle of them all."

The women spent the afternoon looking in the latest bridal magazines for bridesmaids' gowns and color schemes, with sticky notes indicating a nay or yay. Vette didn't feel the need to be a bridezilla.

"Cranberry and cream are my colors. I'll pick the designer and you guys can order whatever dress you want to wear. I'm just glad you agreed to stand up for me. Cyndarella included!"

"I know. She's something else! In actuality, that's a good idea because Denise will be six months pregnant and she'll need to find something attractive, yet comfortable."

"My sister is such a bitch! She told me I shouldn't have Dee stand up because she's pregnant! Of course, Tara didn't stick up for me either, darn it! They are both in love with my fiancé. They can't seem to get close enough to him, now that he's making a legal woman out of me!" Vette confessed.

"Is Tara still dating Lou's friend?"

"Yes, indeed. Of course she had to tell me that he wore her out in bed, and she couldn't keep up with him. She said she told him that sex with her was more of a sprint, not a marathon!" Vette tattled. "She said he modified his plan, and that she's discovered nerve endings in her vagina she didn't know existed!"

The ladies continued gossiping throughout the afternoon before finishing up. Tavie gave Vette the name of her wedding planner who she hadn't had an opportunity to use and again wished her luck.

Chapter Fifty-Three

Greystone Golf Club and Banquet Center in Macomb County was one of Tavie's favorite places to play in the state. World-renowned architect, Jerry Matthews, had designed the eighteen-hole course that included three gravel quarry holes and a beautiful thirty-five acre lake. The rolling hills and magnificent views were an oasis of joy to her, as was the amazing Top of the Hills Grill which had the best Kobe beefsteak ever!

Tavie was playing in the annual Scramble Golf Tournament Classic fundraiser for the Oakland County Teachers' Association, in a foursome with some fellow teachers from the county. The association made money which was used as a financial support for teachers who needed extra money for their classrooms. The state had made many cuts in education and teachers had to be resourceful in creating additional revenue streams to fund their schools.

It was a clear sunny day, without a cloud in the sky. The day was forecasted to be around the mid-eighties, with a possible chance of a thunderstorm tonight. They'd had only a few downpours this summer, and with all the so-called rain prediction theories she'd have to see it to believe it.

Colleagues, retired and present, along with parents and alumni, participated in the well-attended event making it an annual success, although they hoped to beat last year's total which had been$11,000. Tavie was on the organizers', though this year she hadn't been as active as she'd liked to have been, as she'd had personal problems that stood in the way.

Not all the schools in the county had come forward to participate at first, but slowly they began to recruit more by utilizing social media to spread the news, as well as word of mouth. Now they had eighteen schools participating, and that was up five percent on the previous year.

Tavie opened her trunk and gathered her favorite Top Flite Graphite Set, which her father had given her for her fortieth birthday. The clubs were lightweight and easy to use, not that it mattered for a scramble. Some of the golfers had little to no experience, but they came out to show support by sponsoring a hole, or buying a $75 ticket which included a raffle entry, and on-course competitions of the Nearest to the Hole and the Longest Drive. She'd actually had won both in previous years. Her fellow teachers joked that she'd rigged the game to get a prize because she was extremely competitive.

Making her way into the clubhouse, Tavie was approached by Mrs. Hervey, a recent retiree who was also her mentor, and who she was playing alongside this afternoon. Tavie couldn't make Mrs. Hervey's retirement party, but she had presented her with a memorable scrapbook which had over twenty years of mementos that she was able to collect from teachers in various schools the older woman had taught at. It was a contribution that was exhaustive to assemble, but well worth it for Mrs. Hervey, who had carried lots of her personal and professional secrets.

"Octavia, my dear, it's so nice to see you!" Mrs. Hervey said.

"It's so good to see you too! I miss my favorite redhead!"

"Here I am in the flesh. Anytime for you, but you know that, right?"

"Right, Mrs. Hervey. I *know*," Tavie sighed. "We're going to do some damage out here on this course today."

"We are. Is everything starting to settle for you since all hell broke loose with you and Orville?" the redhead asked.

"It is. I'm so glad you told me about Dr. Wiener. She is helping me understand myself better. I swear it seems sometimes that just by hearing myself talk out loud it jars me."

"You're quite welcome! She is a distant cousin, and I knew she'd be of great assistance to you. But it's going to take time to see the kind of progress you need long-term. Don't be too quick to rush it," Mrs. Hervey reflected. "This has been accumulating for years now. You'll make better decisions for yourself in the future." The older woman suddenly recognized someone who would soon put her theory to her test walking up to them, unbeknown to Tavie, whose back faced Mackenzie Dooley as he approached them.

"Good afternoon, ladies."

Mrs. Hervey greeted the man with an embrace, as Tavie quickly collected herself; she was astonished to see Mack.

"Hi, my friend, I had no idea you were going to be here!" she said.

"I know. It was a last-minute thing. Brenda was supposed to come but she had some union stuff to deal with. I came in her place to support the cause."

"I see. We'll have a good game, and I'll see you out on the course. Please excuse me," Tavie said, leaving Mrs. Hervey and making her way over to a group of teachers who warmly received her. Neither Brenda nor Mack had ever attended this event before, but this year his girlfriend had seemed to want to come and check out the former competition, or so she thought, and she hadn't liked it a bit!

When they were alone, Mrs. Hervey gazed at Mack and gave him a piece of her mind.

"You know, Mackenzie, you made your point, but you could've been more tactful. Octavia knows you're off-limits. Behave yourself and stop staring at her, for goodness sake! She has enough men here today, hopefully available, to keep her occupied," the retired woman defended her protégée.

Mack apologized to Mrs. Hervey before he sauntered off. The tumultuous relationship of old needed to stay in the past. Mack and Brenda Barker were an item, yet Mrs. Hervey worried about the undercurrent of anger she'd witnessed in Mackenzie's exchange with

Octavia. He intentionally wanted to hurt her, because even though the man might not have realized it, he was still hurting himself.

Chapter Fifty-Four

Mouna Bazzi spent the afternoon with Cyndarella, showing her how to make her more of her son's favorite dishes. She'd taught Cyn to make Middle Eastern food; and Cyn had proven to be a great learner. However, she had an ulterior move in spending more time with her daughter-in-law. She'd loved how firm yet delicate Cyndarella could be with her children and her son. Bashar respected his wife's opinions greatly, so she hoped this would soften the blow of what was to come.

"Ma Bazzi, this is enough food for an army! We can't eat all of this!" Cyn wailed.

"Invite more family, it will be eaten. Don't worry about it," her mother-in-law remarked. "I want to tell you a story. A not so good story, but for your ears only right now, okay? I have also written it in a letter for you to give to my son upon my death."

"Oh my God! Mouna, are you okay?" Cyn said.

"Yes. Just listen to me. Please!"

Cyndarella felt uncomfortable as Mouna suddenly appeared frail, as if she were about to become ill, alarming her daughter-in-law even more.

"Ma Bazzi, please sit down and let me get you some more Turkish coffee."

Cyn poured them both a refill of coffee and sat down and listened as her mother-in-law continued the conversation.

"My biggest regret in this lifetime was that I did not trust my son not to know his own heart. Ihklas wanted to punish Bashar by sending him to an Iraqi prison where his brother and nephews ran the whole operation." She paused momentarily before beginning again.

"Please go on, Ma," Cyn gently prodded the elderly woman.

"I hesitantly agreed to it—the ruse. Faisal didn't know what we planned for his brother. It backfired. My brother-in-law and his sons were transferred to another prison shortly afterwards, because of Saddam Hussein's band of idiots, and Bashar was tortured because of us," she cried. "Months went by before we found out his brother had been transferred, and the nightmare began. You must tell Bashar for me upon my death. Not one moment before that!" she pleaded.

Time froze for Cyndarella, who was horrified at what she'd just heard. This declaration could destroy her family. She bitterly wept for the young woman she used to be, and the suffering she went through during that time. And she wept for her husband. She ran into the restroom to vomit, but nothing would come out. Mouna brought her a bottle of water and checked to see if she was okay.

Cyndarella cradled Mouna's hands in her face while speaking to her.

"Bashar has to be told the truth about this, Mouna. I mean it. No more secrets. This has gone on for far too long! It's too much!"

"Oh, no, no, no," Mouna struggled. "No! Not now while I'm alive. I'll be good as dead to my son again. Please don't do this, Cyndarella."

"Mouna, I love my husband too much to deceive him any longer than he has been already. I couldn't bear it. You have to trust that he will forgive you. I *hate* what you did to us both, but I *have* to forgive you."

"Oh, my dear, I wish you wouldn't."

"This is the worst day of my life, but it's also the best, because now my husband will learn the truth."

"I swear to God, he'll hate me. And my grandkids will too." Mouna shook like a leaf for a moment, which rattled Cyn even more.

"You are the kids' heroine, *Savta*," she tried to reassure the woman. When translated into English, *Savta* meant grandmother.

Cyndarella was tempted to tell her mother-in-law about the private investigator her husband had hired, but she opted not to, as she was afraid that Mouna would go into cardiac arrest. They were both panicked, and as much contempt Cyndarella felt for the woman right now, she couldn't break up the family they'd become. Bashar possibly would overrule her and she'd support whatever he said. She took Mouna to the in-laws' suite for some rest, as she wrestled with how she'd break the news to her long suffering husband, and how he'd take it.

The Bazzi home had been baby-proofed and fitted out with baby monitors throughout, including the garage, where Bashar overheard the entire confession by his mother. He was crushed, yet relieved it was over. He still loved his mother, yet his father, a man he once held in high regard, had become someone he used to know, someone he now hated.

A man was only as good as his word. Mouna and his father had always promised to protect their children. Bashar was sickened to know to what extent that had meant for them. Faisal would be beside himself as he'd lived with the heaviness of not being able to protect his younger brother; that had been the cross he'd borne for years.

Bashar couldn't have been more proud of his wife's dedication to him. She'd stood her ground with his mother, and had won him over yet again, not that she needed to. Bashar sat down on a stool in the garage to settle himself down, but he knew that he needed to take something for his post-traumatic stress syndrome before he went into an episode.

There was a bottle of Ativan he'd been prescribed that he kept in the glove compartment of his car in case he needed it. He swallowed two pills, and remained in the garage as he chose not to make his presence known at the moment. He couldn't let his wife see him in the current state he'd found himself in, and he was hopeful the Ativan would kick in soon.

Bashar had to get his wife out of the house, for the reason that he needed to confront his mother. The children were spending the day up at Cedar Pointe in Sandusky with their Uncle Pete, grandparents, cousins and anyone else in their group who wanted to tag along, which meant he didn't have to worry the little ones overhearing what was being said. He never wanted them to learn of that brutal time he'd spent in prison, nor the reason why he'd ended up there.

Chapter Fifty-Five

Faisal had come to his brother's home immediately after he'd gotten the urgent call. He didn't know the source of his brother's frustration, which concerned him, for it sounded serious. He hoped it wasn't something to do with their mother, who enjoyed dividing her time between her children's homes. He'd dropped her off to be with Cyndarella and the kids yesterday, and she'd been fine. Faisal drove up the steep driveway and headed to the backyard, where he saw his brother sitting out on the deck.

"Yo, bro! What's up, dude? I'm freaking out! What's going on?"

Bashar relayed the details of what he'd uncovered today about his ordeal from their mother. The blood drained out of Faisal's face and he appeared pale as a ghost. The two brothers resembled each other, though Faisal had begun to recede a bit around his hairline.

"Fucking unbelievable! It's unreal! Our own parents did this!"

The realization blew both the brothers away, as they recalled what had happened twenty-one years earlier.

"I lived with part of my heart being torn out because I couldn't protect you, man, my little brother! How is Cyndarella?"

"Torn to shreds. You should have heard how she stood up to Mom. She wouldn't back down, you know?"

"Where is she?"

"Cyn doesn't know I overheard any of this. When she opened the garage door, I was getting something out of the car and she thought I'd just made it in. She was in a hurry to get to her dance class."

"Man, you think it's safe for her to be out on the road with her state of mind?"

"She was composed, though startled when she saw me. I told her to get going and we'd talk later."

"Where is our dear mother?"

"I believe she is taking a nap. We have to talk to her as soon as she wakes up, and preferably before my wife comes in."

The Bazzi brothers' unfathomable plight left them confused, angry and hurt. They knew their father hadn't taken well to being crossed, and Bashar had challenged his authority.

"I hate our father. I'm glad he is dead!" Faisal spat. "Who does this to their sons? It's monstrous! What do we do about Mom, bro; she's eighty-four, for goodness sake!"

Thunder rang out from the overcast clouds above them and raindrops began to fall. Bashar got up from his chair and led Faisal inside their home through the patio door, where they were embraced by the smell of Middle Eastern fare.

"Man, it smells good in here!" Faisal exclaimed.

Mouna's footsteps could be heard shuffling through the hallway from the kitchen. She appeared and saw her sons.

"My sons! My sons! You're the best in the world!" she said, and hugged and kissed each one of them.

"Cyndarella went dancing at class," she said in broken English.

"I know she did, Mom," Bashar spoke. "Mom?"

"What is it, my son?"

"I heard what you told Cyndarella earlier. I was in the garage and I heard it come through the baby monitor. How could you—the both of you—do it?"

Mouna sat down, bowed her head, and began to sob. Her chest heaved as she tried to speak, but it was almost too much for her to deal with. Faisal sat down next to his mother and held her hand to bring comfort.

"Mom, Bashar and I need to know why you didn't tell us about this before now! Why did you and Dad agree to setting up both your sons?"

Mouna shook as her head and rose from where she was sitting. She looked to the left of her where Faisal sat, and motioned for Bashar to take a seat to the right of her, which he did.

"Mom, I've had many sleepless nights about this. More than you could ever know. Tell me everything that happened. Faisal and I need to be told right now," Bashar demanded emphatically.

"Your father wanted you to help run the family businesses after you finished college. But your second year of school, you got apartment with Cyndarella, and Ihklas wanted to do, like, tough love on you," she revealed, her English a bit choppy at times. "Fadi helped him plan all details, and it got out of hand."

"You used me to do it! Mom, my heart has been ripped out of my chest today!" Faisal shouted. "You'll never know how much guilt I've carried with me about my brother. Never!"

Mouna felt faint, but she would salvage her honor as their mother the best she could and prayed to God they would forgive her in time.

"My heart is broken too! I am sorry for pain I caused both of you, for you mean the world to me! I live with this shame and sadness in my soul for what I did. Always, I do. Please forgive your mother?" she pleaded.

"Mother, it's going to be awhile before I can truly forgive you. I think we've had enough discussion for this for the evening," Bashar replied grimly.

"The same for me as well, Mother. I do love you dearly, but I hurt knowing that Dad convinced you to go along with this plot. You couldn't have talked him out of it anyway."

"Once your father got something in his mind, it was good as done. He never liked to admit he failed. Though once, I got him to admit he was so wrong. Shortly after, he got Alzheimer's. I tell you God punished him for what he did!"

Mouna spent the rest of the evening speaking with her sons over dinner, even though neither of them really had an appetite. Bashar convinced Faisal to take some food home to Samira and his family, because he knew that there was enough food to feed an army, and Cyndarella wasn't a fan of leftovers, no matter how good they were.

"Your wife is okay? She's such a good person, son. Cyn still at dance class?"

"Yes, Mother," Bashar responded drily. "Who else was involved in the scheme other than Uncle Fadi?"

"I swear on my life, not a single person! Only your father and I knew about it. We kept the promise to each other, never to tell."

"Bashar." His older brother took a sip of beer and spoke. "We need to keep this quiet from the others, including your in-laws. Do you think Cyndarella will support us?"

"I don't imagine it should be a problem. She has no idea I am aware of what went down. I need to check on her." Bashar called his wife and got her voicemail.

"Mother, we have to forgive you, but there cannot be anymore undisclosed secrets," Bashar uttered, with Faisal nodding his head in agreement.

"I pray I can die in peace, without taking this home to God when I leave this earth," the deeply religious Mouna affirmed. "I want to know that you both will be okay. Nothing means more than that."

There weren't any more secrets the elderly woman needed to reveal. She accepted the scorn of her sons, yet they were willing to forgive her, and she hoped this would add additional years to her already lengthy life. In the end for her, it was always about God and family.

Chapter Fifty-Six

Cyndarella poured herself a glass of scotch that she quickly knocked back. She needed all the potency of the drink to help relieve the stress of having to rip her husband to shreds with the truth. The thought alone caused her to refill her glass and greedily down it.

The house was quiet, with the exception of the occasional rumble of thunder. She heard the shower running upstairs in the master bathroom. Mouna probably had fallen asleep. Cyn had purposely stayed for three dance classes tonight because she wanted to avoid the woman, who most nights was tucked into bed before 9:30PM. There was a spinach salad in the refrigerator and she took a few bites of it, only because she recognized it was careless to drink on an empty stomach.

Cyn was stood looking out of her kitchen window when she heard Bashar make his way downstairs.

"Hey, love. How was your dance class?"

"Rough, much like the rest of my day," she said turning to face him. "I've got something I need to talk to you about, can we go upstairs? I don't want to wake Mouna."

"You don't have to worry about waking her, she's gone. Faisal took her home. Honey, I was in the garage earlier today. I heard when Mother confessed her sins and those of my father. It came through on the baby monitor."

Bashar comforted his wife as she broke down in tears.

"What kind of parents do this kind of thing to their kids? I'm in shock," she bawled. "I *cannot* believe this shit!"

Cyndarella's reaction didn't sit well with Bashar. She'd been an indirect victim caught in the crossfire of disaster, as he'd been.

"Cyn, listen to me. You're one of the strongest people I have ever met in my life. We can't let this break us, okay? We'll find a way. I promise."

"You're pretty damn brave yourself. I doubt it if I could have survived what you went through," she offered. "I feel really sick. Please excuse me."

The burning feeling in the pit of her nervous stomach made her vomit the small portion of salad she'd just eaten. The taste of bitter scotch residing in her mouth did not help alleviate the issue for her, it only made it worse. A pounding began at her temples and spread throughout her entire head, as a migraine threatened to emerge, further complicating her discomfort.

Bashar placed three cups of fresh berries in the blender, along with plain yogurt, flaxseed oil and a banana, and mixed it up for his wife. The shake had lots of potassium and would help her replenish her electrolytes after throwing up.

Cyn walked into the kitchen, and took the fruit concoction he handed her.

"I have another migraine."

"Let's get you ready for bed." He took charge.

Bashar prepared the shower while Cyn drank the shake. He checked on her as she bathed. He couldn't take any chances on her passing out, as she had once before while she was pregnant with their twins.

Climbing out of the shower, Cyn dried off and oiled her body with organic coconut oil which had a light scent, and which she could tolerate during a migraine, unlike the other heavy fragrant oils and lotions she had in the house. She towel- dried her hair and got into bed without clothes.

"Don't even think about it!" she snapped at Bashar, while pulling the comforter over her head. He was more than willing to use alternative measures to alleviate her tension.

"You'll never know if you don't try," he reasoned, drawing back the cover from his wife and exposing her bare body.

"I'm tired and angry! Why can't you understand that?" she yelled at him.

His mouth claimed hers and he kissed her.

"You've got all night to take it out on me, my love," he stated, as he made his way inside of her to give her some medicine of his own.

Chapter Fifty-Seven

There was never a dull moment in the busy amusement park at Cedar Pointe in Sandusky, Ohio. The whole gang came along for the day, minus Cyndarella and Tavie. The Worthy family was well-represented, with Cyn's parents, nieces, nephews and brother in tow. Vette originally said she couldn't make it, but her kids weren't having it and guilt drove her into coming.

Willa and Vernon had taken the twins to the waterpark side to let them have their own little adventure, for they did not fare well waiting in the long lines for rides. Sean and Pete hung out together, while Denise and Vette managed kid duty and kept everything on track.

"It's good you and Sean came out today with Marla. I'm glad you're working things out."

"We're trying. We've had these really candid conversations with each other."

"How bad was it, girl?" Vette asked.

"Lot of tears and disappointment on both sides, though I did most of the crying. My hormones have got me all out of whack!" Denise laughed.

"Do you think you can trust him again?"

"That's a tall order. I'm trying to like him again. I mean, don't get me wrong; I love the man, but I don't like him right now. I'm getting there."

"He probably feels the same way about you!" Vette joked, as the women laughed.

"You're right! I didn't make it any easier on him. He made me come clean about my junk too! But we're moving ahead and rebuilding our life together with our daughter, son and new home, God willing."

The women continued to wait in line with the remaining children, who wanted to go on the kid-friendly rides. Denise stayed watching while they rode. They decided to eat an early dinner at the food court, where they joined up with Pete and Sean.

"I see my parents are still at the waterpark," Pete stated. "I'm having a blast, but it is getting a little too hot round here for the kids to be walking around."

"I'm thinking the same thing. You want to head over to meet Willa and Vernon where it's cooler?" Vette asked.

"Yeah. We should probably do that," Pete responded.

"We're in!" Sean declared. They finished eating and cleaned up their area in the food court.

"I can't believe it costs over $150 just for hamburgers and French fries!" Marla exclaimed.

"That's grown people's stuff to deal with," Vette's preteen daughter, Carly, stated, making the adults around her laugh.

Pete held his niece, Nadia's, hand, and along with the other children gained entry into the water park where they cooled off. Pete was conservative and did not like to see any young girl in swimwear without adult supervision. There were too many weirdoes in the world in today's times, and he wouldn't hesitate to defend his family if it was necessary. The little girl, with Vette's help, had changed into a yellow ruffled one-piece bathing suit, but he made Nadia keep her shorts on, as he did his own children.

"Uncle Pete, why do I have to keep my shorts on?" Nadia whined.

"They stay on, just like your cousins' are, or we leave. Understood?"

"Yes!" she pouted. The girl was opinionated yet not spoiled, which didn't surprise him. Cyndarella was the only female who would rule the Bazzi household, he thought.

The family enjoyed lots of selfies and picture taking, before heading back to their cars to begin the ride back home. Vette was careful not to get to close to Pete, who she still secretly desired a little, though her infatuation with him was over now that she had finally become engaged. A part of her was disappointed because she'd often wondered if they could have made it as an item. She fought her attraction to him and kept things light. Besides, she really didn't think Pete went out with White women, even though he said he didn't have a problem with it. All she'd ever seen him with were good looking Black women, and she didn't feel like she could compete.

Brent and Carly helped clear out the car when they arrived home. The kids were exhausted and headed up to bed. One thing that had changed throughout the years after she'd adopted the kids was that they both finally could sleep through the night. No more late night refrigerator raids or coming down for snacks; sleep time meant just that. The next morning, Vette looked around and couldn't find her purse. She checked out in the car again, but couldn't find it. Denise didn't have it, and the Worthys weren't answering their phone. She didn't have a cell phone number for them, but she had Pete's.

"Pete. Good morning, it's Corvette," she said.

"I just tried calling your parents, to see if I left my purse in their car during one of the breaks, but no luck. Can you call them and check for me?"

"I'll call you right back," Pete told her. He called his parents' mobile phone in their Cadillac and they indeed had Ms. Vern's purse.

"Vette, your purse has been found. It's in the Cadi."

"I really need it. Can you drop it off, or do you want me to come over there?"

"Vette, you know, I live out in Ann Arbor now, but for you, I'll swing by my parents' house to pick it up for you when they get home."

"Pete, you don't have to do that! I can go and get it from them."

"Do you have an extra driver's license hanging around?"

"No."

"Look, you'll have your purse shortly. Text me your address, alright?"

Vette hung up the phone and texted over her address. She didn't know why she felt so nervous. Brent and Carly were home, so nothing would happen. Mrs. Worthy called her shortly after this, and told her that she and Vernon were at Trader Joe's on Maple at Telegraph, and would deliver her purse, to her relief. Was it just her imagination, or was Pete Worthy intentionally screwing with her mind, or was she the only one doing it all by herself?

Chapter Fifty-Eight

The golf classic once again was a success! They raised $26,000 this year. Tavie noticed the clouds start to take a turn for the worse while she gathered her clubs and loaded them in her car.

Mrs. Hervey spied Mack looking towards the parking lot and at Tavie.

"Storms," he said. "She hates them. That's why she's getting antsy," he said.

"Octavia has always hated hearing the thunder, especially when she's in the classroom with her students."

"It's more like a phobia for her. It's a lot deeper. I want to make sure she's okay before she takes off."

Tavie headed back towards them after she'd said her goodbyes to all the participants. She needed to go home before the downpour started.

"Hey, you won the Hole in One contest. You've got to claim your prize," Mack reminded her, but she shook her head to say no.

"Mrs. Hervey, will you collect the prize on my behalf and I'll get it from you another time?" she asked, while looking up towards the clouds. "Besides, if I leave now, I can catch *Grease* from the beginning," she smiled.

"Not again!" Mack scoffed. "Woman, you still are obsessed with that musical?" he teased her.

"Yes, I am. I can't resist it. And I'm leaving right now. Bye," she waved.

Mack was caught off-guard by thoughts of old. He remembered a day like this, some eight years ago, and the price he'd paid for it.

"Mackenzie, what is it?" Mrs. Hervey asked.

"If you don't mind, I'll take Octavia her prize and see her through this storm, as her friend. I wouldn't be surprised if she crawls into a fetal position under the covers till it passes over, that's how bad it is for her."

"Only if she agrees to have you bring it. And if she does, damn it, Mackenzie Dooley, don't you hurt her, do you understand me?" the older lady warned him.

"Yes, ma'am. This is something I need to do."

Mackenzie confirmed with Tavie that it was fine for him to drop off her prize. She seemed surprised to hear from him, but she agreed. He couldn't make up for that awful night years ago, but at least, he'd stay with her until the storm passed.

TAVIE HAD SHOWERED and changed clothes when the gate attendant buzzed to ask for permission to let Mack through, and she consented. A favorite musical scene of hers was playing on the television and she had it on so loud that she almost didn't hear her doorbell.

"Tavie, really? You can hear the TV in your driveway!"

"I have to drown out the sound of thunder. Come on in," she motioned with her hand.

He came in, and noted the changes she'd made to the place: it looked nice. The gray sofa with yellow accent pillows, along with the abstract paintings that covered her wall, were trendy. He liked it.

"Here's your prize, before I forget." He handed her an envelope.

"I bet it's another gift card. I'll open it later. You gonna watch this with me or are you leaving?"

"I can't believe I'm getting suckered into watching this musical again. Goodness!"

"I'll grab you a beer," she laughed.

They sat on the couch and watched the musical with an awkward amount of space between them. Between commercial breaks, they made small talk.

"How's counseling coming along for you?"

"It's been enlightening. I've learned a lot about myself. I've never really been alone, but for the first time I am and it's not scary like I imagined it would be."

Grease came back on, and Tavie shushed Mack so she could watch the movie. A loud clap of thunder startled her and she spilled beer on her shorts, so she went to change. Mack hoped the storm would be over soon so he could physically get the hell out of there before they did something they'd both regret.

Tavie returned to the family room in another pair of shorter shorts, but seemed unfazed by the effect on him as he watched her.

"Okay, it's that all you have to put on?"

"What are you talking about?"

"Tavie, you might as well be walking around in your panties, as short as those things are!" he laughed.

"You're so nasty! I'll sit in front of the TV so you won't get any ideas!"

A downpour of rain hit upon the house, along with a howling wind, right before the message came upon her television that the satellite had lost its signal.

"Damn it!" she hissed. "I hope the power isn't next."

"Hey, calm down. We're going to ride this thing out until it goes away, then I'll go."

"Busy day tomorrow?"

"Actually, yes. I'm closing on my new house tomorrow afternoon."

"I didn't know you were moving. Congratulations! Where are you moving?"

"West Bloomfield."

"Mack, don't let me keep you. You don't have to stay here with me. Really, I'll be okay," she reassured him.

"You'll always be important to me, even though our lives have gone in different directions. I'm only a phone call away if you need anything. I mean it."

Mack's words threw Tavie as, once again, she was reminded that he had moved on, and it bothered her as she stood up and sat down next to him on the couch.

"Mack, I get it, alright? You've moved on. I'm not trying to be in your way. I just need you to stop throwing it in my face every time you get a chance!" she spat. "I don't want your ass any damn way!"

"You've never been good at lying, Octavia. Stop it!"

"You stop it! I don't need to lie to you!" She got up from the couch, but he pursued her further into conversation.

"What's with the short shorts you got on? Huh?"

"I wear what the fuck I choose to in my house!"

Mackenzie couldn't help but laugh to see her so worked up. He didn't care, as long as it took her mind off the storm. Lightning lit up the room and she shrieked out in fear.

"I like your shorts, actually, they're cute, and you can wear them in your house anytime you want to!"

"Seriously, Mack, you've got to stop acting like I'm trying to jump your bones, or something. I'm not!"

"I'm sorry it's awkward between us. I'm not trying to be a jerk. I don't want to see you hurt again. That's all. Can we call a truce?" he said extending his hand.

"Deal."

Mother Nature had her own mind, and another wave of thunder crashed, as lightning flashed lighting up her home.

"I'm scared. I love summer, but I hate the storms."

"I remember when you said that to me before, eight and a half years ago."

Tavie stood looking out onto her patio from the dining room.

"Mack, I can't go there," she said, with her back facing him.

"Whenever there is a summer storm in the evening or at night, you and the child we lost...I can't help it, it takes me back there. You're the only person I can talk to about it."

"You didn't forget about our—" Tavie couldn't bring herself to say it.

"*Our* baby. No, Octavia, and I never will."

Tavie moved away from him, wiping her eyes. She reached inside her liquor cabinet and grabbed a shot glass and slid back three shots of Crown Royal to help calm her nerves. Mack took the bottle from her and put it away.

"Mack, I had no idea you thought about it, too!" Tavie admitted. She reached up and wrapped her arms around his neck and held onto him. The spell of grief reunited the pair temporarily. The vibration of his cell phone interrupted the mood.

"It's Brenda."

"Go ahead and take the call. I'll leave the room."

"It's not necessary. She wanted to help me with some last-minute packing this evening, that's all," he said nonchalantly, noting the wounded expression on Tavie's face.

"The storm let up. You can leave now."

"Something was happening between you and me before that phone call. I don't know what, but it was rather incredible," he responded, gazing at her intently.

"I felt it too," she concurred, while he stroked her face with his hand. He couldn't end the evening with her without kissing her—that wasn't a crime. The effect she had on him however was deliciously criminal. He used to wonder if she missed him, like he did her, though he stopped doing so recently.

"I'll call you soon, okay? This time, Octavia, damn it; make sure you know what you want."

"Brenda is waiting for you right now, so what I want doesn't matter, does it, Mack? Goodnight."

"Let me deal with Brenda," he tried to bargain with her.

"When you have the time to listen, I'll tell you exactly what I want."

With that said, Tavie shut the door, and it separated her from Mack. He lingered for an instant before he knocked on the door again and this set her heart aflutter.

"I forgot something," he said, as he stepped inside her home.

"What is it?" she asked.

"When you decided to walk away from what we had, it hurt. You didn't want to try anymore, and made sure you let me know that you were happy with your Jamaican—"

Tavie interrupted him. "It's late, Mackenzie, can't we talk about this later?"

"No, I'm afraid not. I called you for over a year before I gave up on you, and before I moved on even to date."

"That's unfair, Mack! You know I wasn't the one who strayed when we were together. You can at least give me credit for that!" Mack was quiet while Tavie gave him a piece of her mind. "You also fucked around with Geneva, a Jamaican, so you need to stop with the double standard shit!"

"I had a fling with that woman. She didn't mean a thing to me. Don't toy with me, Octavia. Neither one of us need drama at this point in our lives." Mack gained his composure and once again departed for the night.

The level of arousal he'd stirred in her caused her to take another shower to wash away the remains of the pent-up moisture that coated her engorged vagina. Love's tendencies appeared much like a board game. You could roll the dice and, depending on where you landed on the board, you either won or lost. There was no in-between and she was tired of being on the losing end! Tavie grabbed her phone and tried calling Cyn, but it went to voicemail. She called her friend's landline, which she rarely did, because she really needed her advice. "Hello," she whispered. "Cyn, are you asleep?"

"Something like that, what's up?"

"It's a long story. Mackenzie was just here, and we sort of reconnected, but nothing happened. Brenda's in the picture now. What do I do?" she whimpered. "Cyn, you there?"

"I'm here," Cyndarella breathlessly answered. "Tav, you've got to take control of the situation. Does he want you or Brenda? First, figure that out. There's no room for errors, alright? So don't waste your time or his until you come to some sort of conclusion. "

"I'm sorry I woke you, Mrs. Bazzi. Thanks for setting me straight, yet again!"

"Go and get him, girl! Goodnight!"

Tavie thought about what her friend said and how she sounded, and became embarrassed when it occurred to her that she might have interrupted the Bazzis' nookie time. Rabbits had nothing on them! Tavie got in bed, and tried to read the latest edition of *Essence* magazine, but she couldn't concentrate on anything on the pages. Her mind raced back to Mack and, as a result, sleep would be hard to come by for her.

Chapter Fifty-Nine

Mack sat in his sparkling black E-Class Mercedes sedan in Tavie's driveway. He didn't want to leave. He noticed that she'd turned off the living room light, which indicated to him that departing was the right thing to do. Comedy Central reruns of The Colbert Report played out on the satellite radio in the car as he began the trek home.

Brenda had called him at least six, unprecedented times tonight questioning him, which did not still well with him. She hadn't acted in a jealous fashion since they'd started dating four years ago. They hadn't become exclusive until the last year and a half. Before that, he'd still enjoyed the company of other women; she'd known about it, and he'd encouraged her to do the same.

A sadness enveloped Mack's conscience. He wanted Octavia more than ever, and the old Mack would have been having his way with her right now, but he'd worked beyond that. He'd almost sacrificed it with her. Mack could still feel her lips against his. And that last hug they'd shared had really fucked him up, because her vaginal secretion coming through on those short shorts had left a damp reminder on his trousers.

Mack parked inside his two-car garage, and closed it. Before he had a chance to get inside the house, Brenda rang the doorbell on the front porch. He was relieved he hadn't given the woman a key.

"Hey, I've missed you today," she said with a big dimpled smile.

"Hello, dimples," he said giving her a peck on the cheek, as she made her way inside his home.

"So, how was the golf game? My spies told me how Tavie was showing off her golf skills, practically throwing herself at all the men!"

"Not true. Moreover, I don't want to talk about Tavie. You came over here to help me pack, remember?"

"You're awfully defensive tonight. Don't tell me you were jealous!"

Mack wasn't in the mood to deal with his mocha-colored lover's insecurities. He didn't like the idea of her toying with him to try getting information about anything related to Tavie.

"Why don't tell me what this is really about?" He spoke with frustration.

"You know what the fuck it's about!" Brenda barked. "You were with her tonight, I just know it!" she accused.

"Brenda, I can't give you what you need unless you tell me what it is you're after."

"Are you sleeping with her?"

"No."

"But you want to, right? Why don't you be a man enough to admit it?"

"It's crossed my mind, but nothing has happened, Brenda, nothing. Drop it!"

"I can't. You see, you remember the day after your little counseling session with that bitch's therapist?"

"What about it?" he asked crisply.

"We celebrated your mother's birthday here, and we'd both drank a lot. When everyone left, you used me, and I hate you for it!"

"What are you talking about?"

"You repeatedly called out Tavie's name when we had sex! You didn't even touch me the same! You were almost like another man!" The fury spewed out of Brenda as she continued arguing. "At first, like an idiot, I thought because of your love for me, we'd moved to another level, but then I realized it wasn't *me* you wanted to be with!" she raged.

Mack reached out to touch Brenda's shoulder, but she yanked away from him.

"Brenda, I wish you would've told me. I didn't mean for that to happen. I've never used you. Whenever we've been together, I've had nothing but love and respect for you."

Brenda paced back and forth in the living room, which was filled with boxes. She didn't want to hand him over to Tavie without a fight.

"I apologize for what I said, but I haven't cheated on you, Brenda," he said remorsefully.

"Let me explain to you what I need from you, so we're clear. We've both invested too much time in this relationship to let it go to waste! It's pretty simple for me. You can't see Octavia anymore, or we're done."

"If you really mean that, it has to be the latter; we're done."

Brenda was licensed to carry a concealed weapon. She grabbed her purse and removed a hot pink revolver.

"I should shoot your Black ass for this shit!" she hissed, pointing the gun in his direction. "But I'll leave before I kill you, motherfucker! I can see myself to the door!" The smug asshole of a man didn't even as much as flinch while he stared at her march out into the night.

Brenda grabbed her keys, made it to the car, and sped off. She knew Mack felt guilty, but it wasn't enough. She'd been married once before, then divorced her husband because he'd preferred being in her company, without too many friends hanging around them, smothering her. She'd never worried about a bitch with him, like she had to do with the rest of these dogs of today. She swore the next man who'd mistaken her for a sucker would take a bullet—and she wasn't bluffing.

Chapter Sixty

The Shenandoah Country Club was hosting a wedding reception for one of the Bazzis' cousins. Nadia had been selected as a flower girl, a role she treasured as she'd had lots of practice! At seven, Cyndarella's daughter had walked down more wedding aisles than she could count.

Cyn had learned some Arabic, but not enough to speak it fluently, though it didn't matter. Most of the people were English speaking, but there were some who conversed solely in Arabic, which left her out of the discussions. Chaldeans partied non-stop like nothing she'd ever seen! She'd been a quick learner, for this was the way of life in with her new family. There was always a shower of some sort, but they weren't like the ones Americans held. The brides were presented with lots of jewelry, money and cars.

The music at the reception was blaring from the speakers as the live band sang *Endless Love* on the stage, serenading the bride and groom. There were some of the best-dressed people dancing and romancing at the reception tonight. Cyn had dreaded coming to the wedding because she didn't want Mouna to watch her like a hawk. She couldn't let her see what a mess she'd become, or anyone else for that matter. Bashar was an exception; he was onto her.

Cyndarella made her way to the restroom after the surf and turf meal was served. She'd eaten a few bites and then excused herself from the table while Bashar was mingling with the guests. The thing about her stomach was that it was unpredictable. One minute, she was fine. The next instant, she'd move heaven and earth to expel everything from her body. She'd lost five pounds in a week, and her husband wasn't happy.

"Cyndarella. There you are! How do you always manage to look so good?" a visibly pregnant Wiyad said.

"Wiyad, I didn't know you were expecting! Congratulations!"

"We kept it quiet on purpose. Too many miscarriages, we wanted to be sure. It taken us nine years to have another baby," Wiyad relayed in broken English.

"I'm excited for you. I'm here for you if you need anything," Cyn said, as they left the ladies' room.

"I need your metabolism. You always stay so trim and fit. I need to borrow some of that".

They managed to walk out of the spacious ladies' room, bumping into Bashar who couldn't help but overhear the comments about Cyn's weight. It bothered him. Nonetheless, he delighted in teasing his cousin about her pregnancy.

"Being pregnant agrees with you. Trust what I say. My wife was so demanding and emotional the whole time. I needed Dramamine to keep up with her moods!"

The family laughed and danced until the wee hours of the morning. The poor twins had to be carried out by their father, and Nadia literally fell asleep as soon as she sat on the car seat. Cyn prepared her daughter for bed, while Bashar got the boys undressed in their room.

Cyn made it back to their bedroom, where she jumped into the shower with her husband. The wedding reception had so drained the energy out of them that sex didn't cross either of their minds; the warmth of the water splashing upon their tired bodies was more than enough for them. Upon finishing their shower, they toweled off and climbed into bed.

"How did I do this evening? I didn't want Mouna to feel uncomfortable."

"You were fantastic! I told Mother you need space now, but it's clear you have forgiven her."

"I am relieved she understands. Faisal is not handling it well, Bashar. He was quite distant with Mouna tonight."

"I picked up on that also. Mother will have to be patient with each and every one of us right now. She in actuality is just happy to be around the family."

"That's not surprising. I mean she's eighty-four years old."

Bashar had to keep a close watch on his wife. In fact, that sole act kept him from going into another PTS episode, though he had slipped a couple of times since learning of his parents' disloyalty. He needed his wife to stay strong for their children's sake. They relied on her; furthermore, so did he.

A family crisis was brewing in the Bazzi household. Cyndarella had lost eight pounds in two weeks, and was becoming extremely frail. The dust of betrayal suffocated her. No matter how hard she tried, she couldn't will herself to shake the sensation of despair to which she had succumbed.

The children came into the bedroom with their mother's favorite fresh fruits on a tray, including pineapple chunks, blueberries, strawberries and cantaloupe. Nadia also made tea for her mother, using her very own little tea set.

"Eat with us, Mommy," Zaid begged.

"We have lots and lots of fruit to make you feel better. Open wide," Zahir directed Cyndarella, placing a strawberry in her mouth which she struggled to chew.

"Now, drink the tea I made, Mommy!" Nadia demanded. "It's green tea. I made it just for you without sweeteners, so it's perfect!"

Cyndarella took in as much food as her stomach would allow. The joy on the kids' faces encouraged her to eat and drink the tea. Bashar left the room to take a phone call from their family doctor, who told him to bring Cyndarella to the hospital's ER where he would be making rounds this evening, so they could check her vitals.

The doorbell rang, and Bashar found his sister-in-law, Samira, along with Faisal who'd come to check on his wife.

"Where is Cyn?" Samira asked. It's not like her to not call me back."

"In bed for now, but I've got to get her ready to go the ER at Huron Valley Hospital. She's not going to be happy," Bashar announced.

"We'll stay here and watch the kids for you if you need us to, or you can pick them up from our place," Faisal offered.

"Is she pregnant again? She seemed fine a couple of days ago at the wedding festivities."

"No, baby, just exhaustion, I'm afraid. Sam, go up and see her, but don't mention the hospital. I was on my way to tell her when you two showed up. Okay?"

The brothers quietly talked with their voices lowered. Faisal felt it necessary to tell Samira about what happened, but his brother wasn't in agreement.

"It's too risky to tell anyone else. Mother is not getting any younger, and we need to keep this between us."

"I feel guilty not telling Samira, and then I look at Cyndarella. Oh my God! She's so sad, man, are you sure she is going to be alright?" Faisal questioned his brother.

"Sooner or later. This hit her really hard, and she's in a pretty dark place now. We both are."

"I'm crushed our parents could stoop so low. But we can't let Father win."

"I have to keep Mother away from my wife until she's stronger. Cyn doesn't trust her, and that's part of why she is sick."

"Can you blame her, bro? I'm having a hard time trusting her myself."

The brothers furthered their discussion in hopes of squashing their insecurities, though it proved to be without merit. They walked up the staircase in time to hear Samira scream out Bashar's name. He raced up faster in time to find Cyndarella passed out in her jogging clothes on the bathroom floor.

Bashar kneeled down next to his wife until she came to.

"What happened?" she inquired.

"We're going to the hospital to find out." Bashar carried his wife's listless body to his vehicle and took her to Huron Valley.

Samira tried to comfort the children who were hysterical at seeing their mother so ill.

"I want my mommy!" both the boys cried in unison.

"Why is she sick?" Nadia chimed in. "It's not fair!"

Faisal decided they would take the children to their house until their parents returned home. It would serve them best to be in a different environment albeit briefly, for the stressful surroundings made them fearful and they needed reassurance that everything was going to be all right.

Chapter Sixty-One

An IV solution was administered to a dehydrated Cyn to replenish her electrolytes. Her sodium and potassium levels were low, and her blood pressure was 99/100, which complicated matters as far as her physician was concerned.

"Well, how is my favorite patient?" he asked her.

"Tired, thirsty, got muscle cramps and I'm freezing."

"You've confirmed what the blood tests show that your hemoglobin is down a few points to nine, which is the reason for the chills. We need to get that up a bit," the doctor said while he continued reviewing her chart.

"Is that all, doc?" she asked.

"I'm afraid not, Cyn. I'm going to admit you overnight for observation. I'm troubled by the lab report, if I'm honest. Earlier this summer when you had blood drawn, you were well within the correct range." The doctor needed to place the patient at ease, for he'd been her primary care physician for two decades, yet he had to confront the inevitable.

"Cyn, it's been over twenty years since you were treated for an eating disorder but you've clearly relapsed. What triggered this and how long has this been going on?" he asked.

Bashar dreaded hearing the words, though he was one of few people who'd known she'd ever suffered with an eating disorder. Willa had informed him after the birth of their twins because Cyndarella became preoccupied with losing the extra pounds she gained during the pregnancy. She'd gone as far as to buy cases of the liquid protein supplement, Ensure, and had drunk them in place of eating a full meal when she was breastfeeding.

He understood, because of his own condition that certain events could be a trigger, and it was the same for her. It was Cyn's way of escaping pain. Bashar kept on listening to the discussion between her and their family physician.

"Less than two weeks, Dr. Youngerman," Cyn thought as she recalled the exact moment she felt the eating disorder sneak back up on her again.

"Have you taken any laxatives, diuretics, or anything I should know about?"

"I've never relied on supplements to manage my weight, nor was I ever over compulsive about it. Dr. Youngerman. I just feel numb and don't want to eat. If I force it, I vomit. Does that make sense?"

"It does. But you have to eat to live, you follow me? Whatever caused this relapse needs to be addressed now. By the way, how many days in the week are you exercising?"

"Six," Bashar answered for his wife.

Dr. Youngerman knew from all indications that stress factors had thrown his patient into a tizzy. He had to be careful to intervene in a way that didn't make the woman feel as if she were under attack. Patients with eating disorders often were in denial about their condition, although Cyn had been fairly open about hers.

"I will release you first thing tomorrow morning. But we need to get you into counseling with a psychotherapist. Is there anyone you need me to contact?"

Shaking her head in protest, Cyn countered with a suggestion of her own. "Dr. Youngerman, I'm pretty active with the Eating Disorder Association's Michigan Chapter, and I have an excellent sponsor. I'll give her a call."

"Sounds good, and start attending the support groups again. I think that'll be good for you. I want to see you in my office no later than next week."

"You got it Dr. Youngerman," Bashar said, as the two men shook hands.

Cyndarella ordered Bashar out of her room so she could get some rest. The biggest impediment was the safety of her children. She refused to have them around his mother without either of them present.

"Please let me get some rest here, and pick me up in the morning with my babies!" she requested. "I know they'll sleep better if they are home with you.

The man, who normally stubbornly refused, ended up complying with his wife, though he felt indirectly responsible for her hospitalization.

"You've only been in the hospital when you were giving birth. Now you're fighting anorexia again. I knew it when I saw you start to move the food around on your plate, or making excuses about why you didn't want to eat."

"Let's not do this here. These IVs actually are making me sleepy. I love you, Baz. We'll finish talking about this tomorrow.

Bashar sat at Cyn's side until she dozed off. He called his brother and told him that Cyn would be home in the morning. Faisal agreed to let the children stay overnight, but Bashar decided that he would spend quality time with his kids. Everyone wanted to 'borrow' the children and he and Cyn were grateful, but their offspring needed to know that he was there for them and their mommy was going to be alright.

Chapter Sixty-Two

The ultrasound technician placed cool gel on Denise's stomach, while Sean held her hand. Both of them were very eager to see the initial close-up 4D images of their son. An emotional Dee lay on her back on the examination table looking at the monitor viewing the first images as the technician ran the electronic device called a transducer over her abdomen, picking up waves and converting them into pictures.

The grainy ultrasound sound wave pictures took a moment to form making the couple anxious. Seconds later, they saw the beating of their son's heart, but his face was turned away from them. The ultrasound indicated that Denise was actually further along than they'd anticipated by three weeks, according to the technician.

Aiming for different angles provided Sean and Denise a peek of what they were looking for as the baby boy turned towards them and yawned.

"Oh, he's so cute!" Denise sighed.

"Denise, he looks just like me! I can't wait to meet our son," Sean boasted. "This is an incredible moment. Incredible!"

The technician helped Dee off the table so she could empty her bladder in the restroom. She'd drunk lots of water to prep for the procedure, and now she finally got a chance to release it. The baby seemed to be stirring and began to move around as if her stomach were a football field.

After she came out of the bathroom, she joined Sean and Dr. Shah who in his office.

"I have some news I want to share with you. The good news is you have a healthy baby on the way. However, you have also placenta previa. Are you familiar with it?"

"No, I'm not," an alarmed Sean admitted.

"I am. Is it when your placenta covers the cervix? My friend, Cyndarella, had it when she was pregnant with twins."

"You are spot on. Your placenta is only partially covering the cervix. There is a chance it will move up as you get closer to your due date."

"And if it doesn't?" Sean asked.

"We have to perform a C-section. We'll gain more knowledge as we monitor the progress of the pregnancy. I want to forewarn you that if it doesn't resolve, we ask that you avoid anything strenuous after the twenty-eighth week, including sexual activity."

"As long as our son is okay, that won't be a problem," Sean said.

"I won't have to be on bed rest, will I?" Denise queried.

"At this time, no. But, if there is any bleeding whatsoever, I need to be alerted, and you will need to head to the hospital. Agreed?"

Sean and Denise marveled over the ultrasound pictures they'd received, and they opted for a little package that would be set to music the next time she had another ultrasound.

"So, no sex after twenty-eight weeks, Sean, with me or anybody else, right?" she nervously joked.

"I'm sure he meant intercourse, Denise. Shit, ain't a damn thing wrong with your hands or mouth," he laughed.

"Freak!" she retorted, as they continued the drive to pick up Marla.

Sean arrived at a new home development in Commerce Township that he'd been checking out online. They needed a new house for their expanding family, and he didn't have time to purchase a home that needed any major repairs.

"Let's check this out," he said as he led Denise inside.

Chapter Sixty-Three

Vette sat and enjoyed a cup of white bean turkey chili at the café inside of Whole Foods Market after her deposition ended in Ann Arbor. She browsed some bridal ideas that Tara and her sister had sent over. Louis's interior designer had been commissioned to sell some of the pieces that she decided to let go of. Louis was a man of his word. He wanted her and the kids with him in an instant, but he wanted everyone to be comfortable in the space his home provided.

Brent and Carly were ecstatic about the impending nuptials, even though Louis hadn't planned on adopting them. He agreed to help her pay for their college studies, and also provide the day to day expenses that came with growing children—which meant lots of dollars these days with all the latest clothes and gaming stations. The fact a male role model would be in their home on a daily basis satisfied her enough.

"Vette?"

Vette looked around her to find Pete approaching her table.

"Gosh, Pete. You 'bout gave me a heart attack. What's up?"

"I thought I'd grab lunch, and then head back to a site we're working on," he said.

"Look at you looking all rugged in your work clothes," she teased. "What is it that you do?"

"You know I'm a landscape engineer."

"Yeah, and?"

"I work for an architect firm and we have a contract with Washtenaw County. Right now, I'm designing the final project drawings and specs for the city of Ann Arbor. What brings you out here?"

"I had a deposition this morning, and I stopped in here for lunch, like you did. Sit down for a minute and join me," she asked.

"How's the family?"

"We're good. The kids are still talking about Cedar Pointe."

"Mine too. They're getting ready to head back to Minneapolis next week and they don't want to go home with Julia."

"Aren't you trying to get back together?"

"I'm trying to be the best friend to Julia I can possibly be for the sake of our kids. I don't know if we were ever that."

"Shit! I thought you knew Julia a long time before you started dating."

Pete laughed at Vette. She hadn't the discernment to know what being subtle meant. "Why you all up in my business?" he asked her.

"Nah, I don't mean no harm. I just thought we were having a good conversation."

"Hate to disappoint you, but there's not really much gossip to tell. We met up at Ferris, and then she decided to make a career out of being a flight attendant. We were on and off, and then we upped and got married. No long engagement. Is that enough information for you?"

"Yes. I'm sorry, Pete, for prying. I feel like we kind of got close since you've been back. Not just me, all of us. It's nice, actually."

"Well, I'm just about finished with my food. I need to head back."

Vette had a lingering question that she wanted the handsome man to answer. The inquisitive side of her couldn't be contained.

"Pete, before you leave, got to tell you. I used to have the biggest crush on you! I know I'm not a sister, but can you tell me did you ever find me attractive?"

"Used to? C'mon, Vette. Your nose is growing. You still have a crush on me. It's cool, I won't tell a soul," he expressed in amusement.

"You ain't shit!"

"Vette, look at Cyn and Bashar. Love don't know color, people do. That's where the problems begin. If you had a bigger booty, I might've tried to holler at you back in the day. You still fine, my friend."

"Goodbye Pete Worthy!" she said, her voice filled with a bit of regret. She hoped she hadn't made Pete as uncomfortable as she'd made herself. There was no question that Vette considered herself a woman deeply in love.

The wedding was four months away and Vette didn't want a bachelorette party or even a bridal shower, she just wanted to be married without ever having to feel like she was good enough in any man's eyes but Louis's. She threw out the rest of her lunch, refilled her iced-tea and, with belongings intact, headed out to her car.

There was a service van parked next to her, and to her delight, once again, she'd bumped into Pete as he was getting ready to drive away.

"Get in," he suggested which she did, as the local sports radio channel played in the van.

"Vette, you're a very attractive woman. And you're taken. I respect that."

"Pete, thank you. I was hoping I hadn't made a fool of myself."

"You haven't, but you got to knock it off before you get people buzzing. We don't need that."

"I won't tell if you don't," Vette replied, and placing her pink lip-gloss stained lips on his, planted a kiss that he didn't seem responsive to.

"I've got you out of my system now, brotha man." She prepared to leave the van, but suddenly turned back and looked directly at his crotch and saw she'd gotten a stir out of him.

"Looks like we've got company," she announced, while making her way over to his lap. Pete looked in his wallet and tore open a condom packet while Vette slobbered on his dick. He removed her head and slid the condom on. Before he entered her, she was already gone, as she straddled him and took control. However, it was short-lived, for Pete slightly repositioned her body at an angle and lifted his hips to apply pressure to her G-spot as he shoved his hardness persuasively upwards, bringing her to a climax.

Vette laid her head on Pete's chest for a moment before arising. She smoothed out the green high-waist dress she wore and sat for a moment, whereas Pete looked down to discover the condom had ruptured.

"Uh, you see this shit here?" he asked, pointing to his penis. The condom broke."

"Damn it! I'm sure we have nothing to worry about."

"You use birth control don't you?"

"I'm having my IUD removed next month. Pete, I'm really not worried."

"So, did you get what you were looking for?" he pried.

"And then some."

"This can't happen again. I respect Louis. He seems like a cool brother. At one point in my life, it wouldn't have bothered me a bit, until I saw another man getting it on with Julia."

"Did you actually see them?"

"Yeah, and so did the whole cabin crew. Julia filmed the act on her iPhone, in addition to actually being caught by one of the other flight attendants, which led to her leaving her job."

"Cyn mentioned something about it. That's awful!"

"Put it this way, Karma will humble your ass, trust me when I tell you that."

The silence between the two lasted as they quietly reflected on what had transpired.

"For what it's worth, I'm glad this happened. You were like my Denzel Washington, a fantasy. I'm done searching and I don't feel empty anymore. In some way, I'm completely liberated, and it feels phenomenal! I can't wait to marry Louis and be done with the chase.

"Ms. Vern, get your wild ass out of my van. I'm outta here!"

Vette felt no remorse for the little indiscretion that had taken place. She hadn't been with another man since 2008. The bitterness she held towards her fiancé was the fact he'd made her wait so fucking long, just to even give her a ring, and that propelled the constant insecurities that made her question everything about what she thought they were as a couple.

The rumor mills were correct about Pete. He was hung like a horse and knew how to ride her. It was purely lust on Vette's part, more so than his, and that fact shamed her. He didn't even offer her a kiss goodbye, not that she blamed him, as he was not the aggressor. She could now focus on her wedding and be a faithful wife to Louis, like she'd previously been as his lover without any distractions.

PETE HAD NO CHOICE but to go to the site to finish up his day. If he'd had his way, he would've showered immediately after Vette ambushed his dick this afternoon. He'd made it a point to never touch his sister's friends before for two reasons. First, his mother dared him, and secondly, his father paid him not to do so. Although, he and Denise had come close to going all the way.

Denise turned him on the most out of the friends. Tavie was a close second, but she seemed flaky. Vette was a flat-ass White girl, whom he never looked at as a woman. He'd never think the same way about her after today.

The friends were always respectful, which was what had surprised him about Denise one day when she'd ridden her bike over to their home, where he was watching syndicated reruns of *The Cosby Show*. His parents were out working, and Cyn was at cheerleading practice.

"Where is your sister?" she'd asked him.

"At cheerleading practice."

"What you doing?"

"What does it look like? I'm watching TV."

"Aren't you going to offer me something to drink? Damn, you're rude!"

Pete recalled getting Denise a glass of grape juice while she sat down on the sofa and began watching the show with him. She had a round face, with wild uncontrolled hair that perplexed him, but she was hot and he told her so. Denise had been the one to kiss him first. They made out on the couch for at least a half-hour. He even got a chance to finger her, but it stopped there. She'd only wanted him to dry hump her the rest of the time with their pants on, which they did until she came, though, to this day, she denied it.

Pete called his sister to see how she was doing as he hadn't heard from her in a few days.

"Hello."

"Sis, what's going on, girl? Haven't spoken with you in a minute."

"Pete, I've been under the weather but I'm much better."

"I didn't know. What's the matter? Baby number four?" he quipped.

"Fuck you, alright? I wish folks would stop saying that! I'm fine now. You ready to send the kids back to Julia?"

"That's what I wanted to talk to you about. They want to stay here with me."

"You got time to stop over for dinner?"

"That sounds great, sis. You sure you're up to cooking?"

"Get your Black ass over here, and let me fret over that," she chided her older brother.

Chapter Sixty-Four

The last couple of days had been some of the happiest days of Tavie's life. The school season preparations were underway as the teachers met to get their classroom assignments. She hadn't requested a change, and thus was able to keep the fourth grade classroom she'd had last year. Everything seemed to settle down, even her heart.

Dr. Weiner had a rare last-minute cancellation, so Tavie was able to get in ahead of her scheduled appointment. There were so many thoughts clogging her head that she needed to sort through, and that required a neutral third party.

"Good afternoon, Octavia. I'm glad we were able to accommodate you today. What prompted your visit here this afternoon?"

Dr. Weiner heard the summation of events which had occurred in her patient's life. Mackenzie and Octavia had experienced a major breakthrough, and each could start the healing process.

"I'm happy, Dr. Weiner. I'm so filled with a joy I haven't had in a long time."

"Why is that?"

"I have a better understanding of who Mack really is, not who I want him to be. He's not as invincible as I thought him to be."

"What does that mean?"

"Mack has never been an open book, truthfully. However, he touched my heart when he told me he thought about the child we lost."

"Do you think of the child as well?"

"I do. It still makes me sad. I mean, I miscarried the same week I found out about the pregnancy, so it was tough."

"I'm sure it was. So, what's next for you and Mackenzie?"

"There's so much I'd like to say to him. He just closed on a new home, so he's been busy with that, but he's coming over in the morning so we can talk."

Dr. Weiner decided to give Octavia a platform of how to stay on track when she did have a talk with her former lover.

"Octavia, I'd like for us to role-play. I will take on Mackenzie's role, and you can be yourself. We can try a couple of scenarios that will help you build the momentum and break the ice."

"Let's give it a shot. Mack, I don't know where to begin," Tavie started.

"Start over, but think before you speak. I want you to think of this as the last hurrah of your relationship. Not that it will be, but let that soak in a little and begin again."

After several attempts at practicing, Tavie finally got the confidence she needed for a face-off with Mackenzie.

Next day, it was a beautiful morning to enjoy breakfast out on the patio. Mack called to tell her he was on his way. She prepared his favorite breakfast of poached eggs with salsa, and English muffins with blackberry preserves. He liked bacon, but she chose to mix things up a bit and cooked chicken- apple sausage.

For simplicity, she stepped into a rayon jersey hi-lo plum dress with a scoop neck from Gap. The straight silhouette fit comfortably around her curves, hitting just above the knees. She accessorized her underwear by wearing white Bali bra and panties, nothing fancy, or anything she'd been planning to show off.

Mack entered the fenced-in courtyard, where he smelled something tasty coming from the home. She'd left the front door open for him and he went to find her.

"Good morning. These are for you." He handed her the bouquet of assorted flowers.

"Thanks!" she said, as she sought out a vase to place the fragrant arrangement in.

"What you cooking up in here? It smells good!"

Tavie and Mack had breakfast, and he took note that she'd prepared the staple breakfast they used to share, along with Whole Foods' organic orange juice and a cup of coffee.

"Octavia, you did your thing on this, it's great. What kind of sausage is this?"

"Chicken-apple, what you think?"

"It's good. I'll buy it."

"Have you moved yet?"

"I have. I'm almost finished unpacking. Do you know I had over fifty boxes?"

"That's a lot of boxes! Well, at least Brenda helped you organize." Mackenzie didn't correct her. No matter how lovely a meal she'd prepared, he had no intentions on going easy on her. He was determined to put her sultry ass in the hot seat to see what she was made of. He knew her heart, but that mind of hers did not completely align with his at times and they'd butt heads as a result of it.

"Lot on your mind, this morning, I see," Mack observed, as Tavie appeared to be drifting somewhere far away.

She turned towards him, and flashed a smile as she perked up. "I can't stop thinking about the other night, which led me to have you come over this morning to finish our discussion."

"You have the floor. Talk to me."

Shifting uneasily in the chair, an apprehensive Tavie looked away again to collect herself.

"The reason I broke up with you wasn't because I didn't love you," she said nervously, shaking her crossed legs. "I wasn't even thinking about *you*. I was thinking about *me*, for the first time in a long time. You had bitches calling our house and texting me on my cell phone. It was crazy. I was exhausted from you dodging my questions about your hoes, like someone dodging bullets." Her voice cracked with pain. She struggled to go on.

"Octavia", he prompted, while stroking her trembling hands. "I'm waiting, honey."

"Despite all your damn dirt, you and I both know I didn't fuck around with anybody! It was always you."

"I never questioned that," he muttered softly. "I know you were faithful to me."

"Orville wasn't an ideal escape option for me at the time, but I thought if I had a sliver of a chance at just being able to laugh again without being humiliated by you in front of everybody, it was worth me trying to give myself a chance to be happy. Does that make sense to you?" she questioned, with a mist of tears gleaming in her eyes.

"It does."

"I respect that you are in a relationship with Brenda now, but I don't want you to be angry at me for the decisions I made in the past."

"Octavia," Mack tried to break into the conversation but she held up her hand, stopping him.

"Let me finish," she commanded.

"Go ahead, babe."

"We shared so much together, and in that time it wasn't all bad. We had good times too! For what it's worth, Mackenzie, I only wanted to appreciate and love you on whatever journey this life had to offer us together. I did that. And even though it hurts like hell to lose you completely, I did my best and don't have any regrets," she stated fiercely.

There was a time in his life where he couldn't have cared less about seeing a woman cry—even his mother. But that had now changed. It tore at him to see how much pain she was in.

"I can't say the same, Octavia. I do have regrets. I never thought you'd actually leave me."

"Because you knew I was madly in love with you."

"You're right. " He said, nodding his head in agreement. I took you for granted, babe. By the time you had the miscarriage, and we split afterwards, I knew I had to work on me."

"And you did."

"But you didn't trust me, or think I was capable of changing. That hurt me, Octavia. I won't lie to you," he spoke with his brow lifted, and his gazed focused on the only woman in his life who he truly gave a damn about. "Change can only happen if you're willing to do the work, and I was. Even after you were gone, I continued to work on me."

Tavie winced when she heard his declaration.

"Brenda is a lucky woman," she spoke flippantly and sighed. "I'm sure she knows that."

"How do you feel now you've got everything off your chest?"

"Honestly, I am glad you've found someone who makes you happy. But I'm pissed at the same time because it should've been me, and not her. But that's my ego talking. I'll get over it" she grinned. "I need to clear this table."

Mack helped Tavie clean up and he sat next to her on the sofa.

"Octavia, come sit on my lap so I can talk to you."

"Are you kidding me?"

"Just for a second. Relax. I won't hurt you."

"Fine," she replied and cautiously sat on his lap, turning to face him.

"You said something earlier that I need to clarify that I think we can both agree on."

"What's that?" she whispered, looking at him bashfully.

"I am ecstatic I found a woman who not only makes me happy, but who I really love. I'm glad I have your support," he said, as Tavie squirmed and tried to get off his lap. But he clamped down on her which held her in place.

"Mack, please! Now you're being cruel!" She started to get emotional and turned away from his glance. "I don't want to listen anymore about your love for Brenda! I get it! You've chosen her over me!" she spat, wiping the watershed of rapid tears that fell from her eyes.

"Octavia, Brenda and I are over."

The announcement baffled an already anxious Tavie, who was on the verge of collapsing.

"Whoa! What the hell? What happened?"

"You happened."

"I don't understand. You just bought a house—"

He cut her off. "Octavia, I think you know what I'm trying to say, if you'll let me."

"Okay," she sniffled.

"We can't change the past, and all the suffering that came with it. But what we do in the future is totally up to us."

"You're so right."

"There have been detours and all, though we're back on track now, right?"

"Um, hmm. Oh God, Mackenzie, you've really chosen me?" she asked, stunned by what was happening.

Reaching inside the pocket of his linen jacket, Mackenzie pulled out a box. Tavie almost fainted in anticipation when he handed it over to her, for there was no way for her to have seen this coming.

Octavia's hands shook so much she could hardly open the box. Her heart raced and she felt as if she was in a dream. These kinds of things just didn't happen to her.

"I'm over forty, so I'm not getting on my knees to propose to you, but I think you get the picture. Are you going to marry me, woman, or what?"

Tavie was overcome with joy at the sight of the Royal Asscher cut diamond engagement ring. It was the same ring from Nordstrom's that she used to place a picture of on the refrigerator door to encourage him to buy her one when they lived together. The crown style, 2.98 total-weight carats had a diamond split band in fourteen-carat white gold with a round diamond.

"How long have you had this?"

He reached into his jacket again and gave her the receipt, which read September 2, 2008. "I have the certificate of authenticity back at my house, well I mean, our house now."

"You've been carrying the ring around all this time? Why didn't you ask me then?"

"You stopped taking my calls, remember?" I had it all planned out. I took your parents out with my mother and sister and showed them the ring. They were beside themselves at the time," he recalled.

"You told my parents? They never said anything to me about it."

"I begged them not to. You were pretty stubborn about moving on."

"Mack, I'm so embarrassed! You sure you want to marry me?"

Mack reassured Octavia he wanted her to be his wife. She threw her arms around his neck, hugged him and said, "Yes!"

Mack managed to pull away from her embrace for a moment.

"I need you to clear your schedule for the next four days. Go and pack," he ordered.

"Where are we going?"

"We're going to Las Vegas to get married. We leave in a couple of hours, so get going, and bring your gown."

"Really? Like right now?"

"Yes. Go pack!"

Tavie grabbed her garment bag and filled it with several nice dresses she could wear in Vegas. She also threw two swimsuits in the suitcase that she hadn't worn before. Cyndarella told her that she never wore the same swimsuits or lingerie for different men. She always started fresh because she thought it was bad Karma not to do so. Tavie felt compelled to do the same. That meant she would have to buy lingerie in Vegas because she'd worn everything she'd owned for Orville. Thank goodness she had at least a pair of new panties and a bra she'd caught on sale at Macy's!

They arrived in Las Vegas at the Bellagio, where Mack had ordered the honeymoon suite for them. The two showered and changed to go down to dinner. Tavie tried calling her parents when they first arrived at the hotel, but she didn't get an answer at their house or on their mobile phones. She hung up with a forlorn look on her face.

"What's wrong, Octavia?" Mack asked out of concern for his fiancée.

"I can't reach my parents. I know there's a time difference, but I want to share our news with them. Did you tell your mother and Jade?"

"I did. They're excited for us."

"I'm an only child, and I wish my parents could be here with us. Can we have a small ceremony when we get back home for just family and friends?" she asked.

"Absolutely! On top of that, you can buy a new gown, this time one you chose to wear specifically for *me*!"

"Alright. Consider it done," she giggled.

"Let's head down. We have a reservation at Picasso."

Hand in hand, they made it down to the restaurant, where they were led by their waiter to a table—where none other than her parents, Jade and Mrs. Dooley sat waiting for them, causing Tavie to squeal with glee as she hugged everyone at the table and began to cry.

"Come on, baby girl, what are you crying for?" Mrs. Slade asked her daughter.

"I'm so happy to see all of you. I've been trying to reach you all day!"

"I kept her in the dark about you being here," Mackenzie shyly said.

"That's alright, son," Mrs. Dooley said. "It took you long enough to get to this stage in your life, but I wouldn't miss it for anything in the world. Your parents and I have booked the East Chapel here at the Bellagio, and the ceremony will take place tomorrow at 5:15 P.M. We have a lot to do between now and tomorrow."

"And I'll finally have a sister," Jade said as she hugged Tavie yet again.

"Jade, you will indeed gain a sister," her mother agreed. But Mrs. Slade is correct, there's a lot for us to do. Starting with a little shopping here to get some last minute things you'll need for your honeymoon. Then, you'll need to get some rest. We have to meet with the coordinator to discuss what kind of personal touches you'd like to incorporate to the nuptials."

"Mr. Slade, it looks like it will be just you and me," Mack said.

"I think that sounds great. You're marrying my daughter after all. I can lay down the rules about my baby girl here over some stiff drinks, and then we can hit the slot machines," the older man replied.

"Daddy, behave!" Tavie cajoled.

"Of course, you'll have another ceremony when once we get home. I've spoken with Junior and he agreed to perform it," Mrs. Slade affirmed.

"We'll do it at the Wabeek Country Club on the third Saturday in September. I checked and it's available," Mrs. Dooley announced.

The evening passed by, along with lots of animated conversation and celebration between the families. The women decided to take Tavie shopping at the Forum Shoppes at Caesar's Palace to make sure she had everything she needed for the wedding.

"We've got to make sure you're ready, though knowing my brother, he probably would like to have you wear nothing," Jade whispered, but it was still loud enough for the others to hear.

"I still need lingerie for my honeymoon! I have *nothing*," Tavie complained, causing both Mack and Mr. Slade to almost choke on their beverages.

"That's enough, Octavia and Jade! What you trying to do, give me a heart attack!" Mr. Slade pretended to choke, clutching his chest. "You ladies can deal with that!" The other guests laughed.

The ladies whisked Tavie away after dinner and they shopped, which was the ultimate gift for her. She found an elaborate white bridal lace chemise with underwired cups, a scalloped lace trim, satin bow details with detachable garter-belt straps and adjustable shoulder straps in a size medium. Jade spotted a white G-string and white stockings to complete the outfit.

The mothers went in search of additional gifts for the bride-to-be, who couldn't believe how her life had moved on, though she wouldn't change a single thing about it because their families were here and she couldn't be happier. Octavia and Jade snuck off to a local jewelry store close by to find a ring for Mack. Tavie knew his ring size, but she was unsure of what kind to get him. "You know my brother doesn't like all that bling. It reeks ghetto to him. He's a Republican too, and getting more conservative by the day. The only reason he voted for Obama was because he was Black, and he truly thought he'd make a difference."

"Ooh, don't get me started about the gridlock in Washington. It's a damn shame!"

Tavie called out, "Jade, I think I found one!" She pointed to a Tacori platinum diamond band ring. The salesman told her that it was a popular selection and they did onsite sizing, and he could have it ready in the morning and delivered to her room over at the hotel, to which she agreed.

"That's perfect. He'll love it because it's traditional and the round channel-set diamonds are subtle. It's him."

The women met back up with the mothers, who had shopped 'til they dropped and were ready to retire for the evening.

"Octavia, we're meeting downstairs tomorrow for a light breakfast, then we have a spa day planned, in which we can do something with your hair. I'm surprised to see you with extensions," Mrs. Dooley proclaimed. "You always liked the shorter do's previously, though the length compliments you just as much. I'm sure you'll look beautiful!"

"With the summer we've had, I wanted as little maintenance as possible," Tavie explained. "Mrs. Dooley, I want to thank you for helping Mackenzie organize this wedding. I'm so grateful to all of you!" The two women hugged.

"I know you are, sweetheart, and I'm delighted to be a part of this. Mackenzie loves you very much, young lady!"

"And I definitely feel the same way about him. I will be the best wife and daughter-in-law I can be."

"I think we all can testify and say amen to that," Mrs. Dooley testified. "Works for me!"

Jade and Mrs. Dooley headed up to their room, while Tavie decided to have a quick nightcap with her mother.

"Your mother-in-law to be is something else. She arranged for our flights and all, which your father and I were cool with. We split the fuel costs on a charter plane that belongs to one of her friends."

"I like friends like that. Cyn did the same thing for me and Vette, remember?" "Minus the fuel costs though."

"I do. Octavia, are you okay with all of this? It's happening really fast."

"I wouldn't have it any other way. I really love Mackenzie, Ma. And he loves me! I can't imagine going through life any longer without him."

"That's sweet Octavia. Savor this moment, dear, for it won't always be this way. Your job is to fight to keep it as close to this as possible, and you'll always be together, no matter what."

"Aw, Mom, thanks for keeping me grounded."

"Somebody has to deal with Mack's mother, girl! Shit, I need me another drink! I do like Mackenzie, and I am so glad that your plans fell through with the Dread man! I never did trust him!" her mother scoffed.

"I *know*, Mom. You never did stop warning me not to trust him. We need to get some sleep because I want to look my best tomorrow, 'cause I'm getting myself a husband," she sang.

"They're sneaky, that's why! C'mon silly, let's go up after I finish this drink."

Tavie couldn't wait to get back to the bridal suite to make love to her fiancé. He had fallen asleep, but he held her off when she woke him up.

"We might as well wait until tomorrow night."

"Forget that!" she balked. "I want you naked right now!"

"Sorry. I'll be the chick tonight, and politely decline. But tomorrow night, you'd better be A-game, because legally I'll own your ass, and you better be able to hang with me!" he joked.

"I'll hold you to it! Shit, you better be able to keep up with me!" she challenged. The two shared a kiss and ended their long night.

"I CAN'T BELIEVE WE'RE married," Tavie said in awe, after exchanging vows with her new husband. Mackenzie stared at his bride, who wore an Allure satin wedding gown that featured a plunging neckline, unique cutout back and Swarovski crystal accented floral belt.

With her hair pulled to the side and flowing curls coming down her shoulders, she couldn't have looked lovelier to everyone who witnessed the marriage. Mack discouraged Tavie from posting anything on social media because he thought it would be tacky to do so until they'd had a chance to go home and formally make the announcement to their friends, who they knew would be briefly disappointed they couldn't be present at the wedding to support them.

Mack wore a Calvin Klein black tuxedo that he'd purchased, with a crisp white shirt and a red rose in his lapel. The hotel's photographer took group pictures and captured the ceremony, including an intimate first kiss, while the tech team made sure to use the highest caliber of equipment to ensure they'd look amazing in the video, in addition to have clarity in the audio.

The weather outside was one hundred and ten degrees, and it felt great to be inside the beautifully decorated, air-conditioned private dining room where they had dinner with their family.

"I don't know why weddings make people cry!" Mrs. Dooley cried out. The distinguished dark-skinned woman had her partially gray hair cut in a blunt style that feathered and tapered neatly around her ears, flattering her square shaped face.

"At least they're tears of joy, Mother," Jade spoke softly. "Octavia, you're breathtaking! You and my brother..." She choked up before continuing. "I love you both."

"Sis, thank you." Mack shared a special moment with his Jade. "We love you too! On behalf of me and my beautiful bride, thank you so much for coming here to support us, even though it was short notice. I couldn't let this woman get away from me for a second time, so thank you again for your patience and understanding."

There were drinks and food aplenty, to go with the champagne toasts from family. The hotel had even sent over a bottle of champagne on the house, which was a nice added touch.

"I'm so happy, I feel like dancing!" Tavie revealed.

"Save your dancing shoes a little longer and I'll hire the best band to play at the next wedding!" Mrs. Dooley proclaimed.

Mrs. Slade got emotional as her husband raised his glass to toast their only child and their new son-in-law.

"Mack, and Octavia. You're no longer two; today you've become one. In thought, hope, love and spirit. As happy as your hearts are today, don't forget the journey that bought you here. May God bless and keep your union sacred for all time."

"Damn, not only is your daddy Billy Dee Williams fine, but he can give a hell of a toast!" Jade broke in with her overbite smile and her short pixie haircut, reminiscent of Anita Baker's earlier years. "Mrs.

Slade, you know you got a keeper!" the young woman relayed, as the small group laughed.

Mack whispered in the bride's ear to see if she was ready to retreat to their room, and before he got her response, she emptied the glass of champagne in her crystal flute, stood up from her chair, so that they could politely excuse themselves.

Mack opened the door to their suite and the mood of love was set by the trail of red rose petals sprinkled on the floor and bed which was warm and inviting, setting them up for an intimate night of marital lovemaking. The smell of scented candles lit throughout the room sharpened their senses, enhancing their passionate desire. The bathroom also had a complimentary basket of Karma Sutra assorted massage oils next to the Crabtree and Evelyn bath toiletries to help make it a night to remember.

Mack helped his new bride out of her gown. The sight of his new bride outfitted in a white camisole, garter-belt, white thigh-high stockings and white high-heel sandals, sporting a big smile on her face, got Mackenzie Dooley's motor running.

He'd undressed himself, and unhooked the clasps on the camisole freeing her breasts. She placed her arms around his neck and drew him in for a prolonged, saucy kiss, while he ran his hands up her bare legs until his fingers reached her buried treasure where he couldn't wait to place himself inside.

Tavie began to move her mouth down the sides of his neck, as she was hoisted over to the bed where Mack carefully laid her down.

"Did you miss me?" she asked.

"All the time, baby. God knows I did. You missed my Black ass too, didn't you?" he countered. Before she could respond, they began orally pleasing each other dually in the sixty-nine position. Tavie drew in deep breaths, and with each suckle of Mack's fullness she engulfed him in her steady mouth. He pulled her panties aside and repeatedly gobbled her pussy, licking it in a circular fashion, in addition to flattening his tongue to apply pressure to her clit causing her to detonate her juices all over his lips.

Mack sat at the edge of the bed, where Tavie straddled him while wrapping her legs around his waist and began letting her hips do the talking against him, as he supported her back with his hands and at the same time joined her in the movement. Between steamy kisses his mouth found her nipples, which he showered with equal amounts of love, causing the purse of Tavie's love to constrict from the rapid pounding of her husband's straightened arrow.

Tavie began biting Mack on his neck and on his shoulder, and he grimaced from the sensation. His dick felt like it had a separate heartbeat from the rest of his body. His new wife was lost in the throes of ecstasy—that was evident by the plastered look of love on her face as incoherent expressions of passion escaped her lips.

"Ooh! Uh, Uh!"

"This pussy is mine forever!"

"Always," she yelled out. "I love feeling you inside me. Fill me up and welcome me home, baby!" Mack grabbed and squeezed Tavie's ass as she sat astride him. They continued loving each other without interruption before reaching the pinnacle of absoluteness.

The couple took advantage of the small amount of time they had on their honeymoon, and drank a bottle of champagne and shared a hot shower together. Mackenzie quietly was pleased that Orville hadn't stretched Tavie's pussy out. She'd missed him as much as he'd longed for her. He watched her sleeping so peacefully beside him in bed, right where she belonged. They hadn't a chance to discuss birth control, nor had he bothered using a condom. His manhood began to stir with arousal.

Mackenzie placed himself between Tavie's parted thighs, aiming right at her center. He kissed her gently and she slowly opened her eyes.

"I love you, Mrs. Dooley."

"I love you too, Mr. Dooley," she giggled. You want some more?" she asked.

"I want more of you, more of us. Let's see what we can do to make us a baby, if that's alright with you?"

Chapter Sixty-Five

"You like it?" Cyndarella asked, nervously anticipating Bashar's response.

"Are you kidding? I fucking love it! What's not to like? You looking one hundred per cent gorgeous, scantily clad on a custom oil canvas is a treat I will forever treasure."

"Thanks, babe. It was hard trying to find the right anniversary present. I wanted it to be something special. I have one more present for you after dinner," she cooed.

"Well, I think you'll love your present too, but you're not getting it until later on this evening."

"Any hints?"

"Not on your life, sexy!"

"Fuck!" she groaned.

"You know you turn me on when you talk dirty like that!" The couple shared share a quick smooch.

Bashar watched his wife while she organized the children's overnight suitcase for the evening. Despite the slight setback, Cyndarella had bounced back with a vengeance and was healthy again. The support group out in Ann Arbor helped her get back on track at weekly meetings.

"Why are you staring at me like that?" she questioned, as she met his inquisitive gaze.

"Because I can," he kidded. "Cyn, I'm proud to be your husband, that's all. I'm so filled with pride with how you attacked the whole eating disorder thing." She zipped the suitcase, and headed over to her husband to share a private moment.

"I'm proud of you, too! Post-traumatic stress syndrome is difficult to manage when it flares up, but you stick with your counselor to help guide you when you need to."

"Counseling helps a great deal, as do the meds if I need to take them."

"It's ironic we have similar disorders, and the same stressors are triggers for us both," she rationalized. "I love to eat, until a crisis comes, and then I escape."

"I know. But the key is you admit it and we can reduce our exposure to the triggers."

"Like Mouna—and I have to hand it to her for backing off and giving us space—it helped both of us tremendously."

"She's fine in small doses. We'll limit the sleepovers until we both agree we're ready for that again."

"The kids miss having their time with her though, so we have to make a decision soon."

Nadia and the twins charged through the den into their bedroom shouting, "Happy anniversary!" to the tickled parents, who thanked their children with hugs and kisses.

"We have a present," Zaid said.

"But you've gotta come to my room to get it," Nadia directed.

"Like, right now!" Zahir demanded.

Nadia and the twins led the way to Nadia's room, where a gift-wrapped box was placed on her dresser, next to three envelopes. Nadia handed the gift to Cyndarella, who reached towards her daughter to retrieve it.

"Here, Mom, you open the gift."

"And Daddy, you can open our cards," Zahir said.

The lovely framed picture of the children standing on the beach while they'd vacationed up in South Haven was a memorable memento of earlier in the summer.

"This is lovely," Cyn replied, as she and Bashar admired the images of their children in the picture.

"Aunt Samira took the picture of us, and Grammy got the frame for it," Nadia said.

"We love it!" Bashar declared. Afterwards, he read the homemade cards the children had prepared for them, while they beamed in reaction to their parents' response.

The Bazzis enjoyed their morning and part of the afternoon with their children, before Bashar went to drop them off at his in-laws. Nadia was thrilled because she helped her mother choose the outfit she'd wear for dinner.

"Mom, you'll look really pretty in that outfit tonight. Daddy will love it!" her daughter smiled.

"I'm sure I will," Bashar replied. "I'll be back in a while. Please be ready. We can't be late this evening." Bashar barked his last orders, as he rounded up the twins and drove off to drop them off.

CYNDARELLA HAD THE color of both her hair and extensions retouched at the salon. The stylist blew out her long voluminous mane, created a side part with a bang over her left eye for a dramatic effect, and curled her locks with volume at the end to balance out her feminine facial features.

The patrons of the salon admired the hairdo as it came together. Cyn was in a good mood, but the salon could sometimes be a real challenge for her, because the women there were like mini communities of friends who thought they could ask you just about any personal thing for as long as you sat in the chair.

"Girl, I got to get me some of what you're wearing. Is it Remy hair?" a bystander asked.

"You have to ask Linda. I don't keep track of what she puts in my hair because I change it so often," Cyn replied.

"It's expensive, but she's worth it," Linda asserted.

"Does it shed? I wear Bohemian hair, and it sheds all over the place!" the woman continued.

"Are you talking to me?" Cyndarella asked. "Or Linda? I don't know what Bohemian hair is."

"It's that cheap shit!" Lucy, one of the stylists in the salon, laughed. "Girl, you better stop bothering Ms. Cyn. Honey, she ain't got time for stupid questions!"

"Oh, she's the one that's married to that Arab." The woman mispronounced the word phonetically, by saying Ayrab. "I'm thinking about dating somebody outside of my race. I was wondering if White men had big dicks."

"I'm not married to an Arab. I'm married to a Chaldean of Middle Eastern descent. I know it may sound a little bit confusing for you. There is a distinct difference between Arabs and Chaldeans."

"My bad. It's the religious stuff, isn't it?"

"That is correct."

"You're lucky. These Black men out here don't know the meaning of commitment."

"I can agree with some of that," Lucy said. "Though not all of them."

"That's about the size of it," Linda agreed. "They get a conscience after you dump their asses! I'm glad my single days are behind me!"

"Hey, speaking of size, Ms. Cyn, so what can you say about White men, or different nationalities, as far as their packages go?" The annoying woman started at Cyn again.

"Every man is different, so don't believe the stereotyped theories. Most likely, they'll be wrong. And another thing," she continued. "Instead of wondering if you should date outside of your race to find love, make sure that it's not just a Black or White man, it's the *right* man," she emphasized.

"The lady has spoken some words of wisdom," Linda said. "In addition to subtly telling your customer to shut the hell up!" she said to Lucy, as the women roared with laughter.

Linda snatched off the plastic cape from Cyndarella's shoulders, and twirled her chair around to face the mirror.

"Happy anniversary, Mrs. Bazzi. Did I do the damn thing, or what?" she said.

Cyn responded with a resounding "Yes!", as Linda helped touch up her makeup. She presented her credit card to pay, but Linda wouldn't hear of it.

"It's on me. You've been coming in here almost every week for over a decade. Enjoy your day!"

"You can at least let me tip!" Cyn implored.

"Goodbye, Cyn. Give that handsome husband of yours my regards. Tell him I said, don't send you back up in here looking like Buckwheat from sweating your hair out!"

"That's the reason for the extensions, remember?"

The women enjoyed a few more moments of ribbing, then each continued on with their day.

"DAMN, LOOK AT YOU!" Bashar flirted with his wife, who wore a Hi-Lo slinky, textured, metallic maxi dress that had a V-neckline in the front and a T styled back. The hi-lo hemline added a sexy flair to the dress and accented her gold and silver Bandolino leather and metallic sandals.

"It's pretty hard to get dressed up when you don't know where the hell you're going, Bashar!" she chided. "Wow, my man! You're looking pretty damn good up in here, love!" she added, causing the handsome man to blush.

"We'd better get going," Bashar completed her thought.

"Or we'll never make it out of here!" they said in unison, laughing.

HER HUSBAND WORE A Michael Kors olive-colored linen suit and a white shirt. The suit was one of her favorites, for she loved the fit of the jacket with a notched lapel, four-button cuffs and front flap pockets. The pecan-toned Oxford shoes polished off his outfit, and he looked incredibly handsome.

"I wish you'd tell me where we're going!" she pleaded to her husband, but it fell on deaf ears.

"You'll see soon enough," he said, as the limo driver proceeded onto I-96.

The couple sipped champagne and discussed their day while driving towards a destination unknown to Cyndarella. The only thing she knew was it involved an overnight stay, and Bashar had had the decency at least to share that tidbit of information with her. She couldn't wait to see what he had chosen for her anniversary gift. She wondered if it were jewelry of some kind, or another vacation to some exotic location.

THE DRIVER HEADED EASTBOUND onto I-94, when Cyn started to figure out where they were headed.

"I can see the wheels turning in your head and I ain't saying anything."

"Okay. If it's where I think it is," she squealed, "I'm so excited!"

The limo driver pulled into Jefferson Beach marina, which delighted Cyn.

"This brings back such good memories for us."

"I know. It's our spot," he acknowledged.

The driver opened the door for them, after he got their overnight bags out of the trunk, and they walked over to the yacht where the crew members were waiting for them.

"Mr. and Mrs. Bazzi, good evening! Climb onboard, and let's get you guys some champagne. I understand you're celebrating your anniversary."

"We are. The seventh to be exact," Bashar responded.

"I'm Joshua, and I'll be your captain for the duration of the excursion. By the way, you two look familiar. Have you chartered with us before?"

"As a matter of fact we did, roughly seven years ago," Cyn said hesitantly, as embarrassment washed through her and she remembered their previous stay. She had a set of pipes on her and she knew everyone had heard them fooling around.

"Yes, yes, I was onboard back then as well," Joshua said, as they got reacquainted on the fifty-seven-foot luxury yacht. "It's hard to forget such a good-looking couple! I have a good memory," he bragged. "For sixty, you know?" he wisecracked. "Rosa will be your server for the evening—she is my wife as well—to make this a special evening for you."

Cyn and Bashar hung out at the back deck and shared drinks and appetizers.

"I'm so embarrassed! He remembered us!" she sulked.

"He remembered your loud ass. I think everybody out on the water that night got an earful."

"Thanks for the vote of confidence!"

As they sat at the bar, Bashar and Cyndarella enjoyed looking out onto the St. Clair River. It was a romantic yet hot evening. The temperature was ninety-two degrees and it was sticky. The nice breeze cooled them off.

Bashar reached down into his bag, pulled out a flat box and handed it to his wife.

"Happy anniversary," he said, and kissed her on the cheek. He watched as she removed the ribbon and opened the box. She opened the document and couldn't believe her eyes.

"Oh my God! This is the deed to our home."

"Yes. I paid our house off."

"Oh, Bashar," she said hugging him. "When?"

"Business has been good, you know that. I closed some big deals, one right around the time you weren't speaking to me because of that little altercation."

"Honey, this is really incredible!"

"Well, our goal has always been to become almost debt free by reducing as much of what we owe as possible. Now we can concentrate on something else."

"You make feel so secure, Baz. I don't know how I can ever thank you for being who you are."

"You never have to thank me, love. Everything I do is for our family. It always will be, no matter how many mood swings or tantrums you and the kids may have," he joked, before getting serious again. "I'm in it to win it."

Cyn became emotional, for she remembered what her life had been without him, and it was hard to believe that, despite the detours, she was back where she started, and the amount of devotion she felt towards him became hard for her to contain at times.

Rosa came over to them to ask them when they would be ready to have dinner served, but they were in a passionate clinch, and the woman decided it would be best for her to come back once they gathered themselves. She'd remembered the pair. The man had seemed easygoing, but the woman was uptight, almost guarded, though the drinking changed her, loosened her up that evening all of those years ago. She got a feeling their lives had changed somehow, but she didn't know to what extent.

They went into the private stateroom, but Cyn told Bashar he needed to leave and come back in about ten minutes because she had a surprise for him too. She directed him to tell Rosa they'd be ready for dinner in an hour. She quickly changed into her sexy two-piece black racer back halter top with a ruffled mini skirt. She got out her iPod and place it onto the Sony alarm clock docking station in the room. She practiced her routine in the mirror, digging the sexy moves Libby had taught her.

Cyndarella found her song on the anniversary playlist she'd created of all the songs they listened to from back in the day to the present. Bashar was instructed to knock on the door before entering, and he did, to see his wife looking like a sexy go-go dancer. She had a chair placed in the middle of the stateroom that he sat in while she performed a hot number to one of Maxwell's sexy tunes, though he couldn't make out which one, for he was captivated with her body's sensuous moves that caused his dick to inflate so robustly, it pressed up against his pants and threatened to burst them in anticipation.

Bashar also received a lap dance and he could feel the humidity coming from under his wife's tiny little skirt. Clothing was removed as Bashar guided her to the bed. It was her night and he would give in to whatever she wanted, which soon became evident. As Bashar lay on the bed, she straddled his face, placing her pussy over his mouth. Her back arched backwards, as she played with her tits while he satisfied her.

Cyndarella panted in short bursts of delight as she came to climax numerous times. She kneeled before him and gave his dick a tongue-lashing he wouldn't soon forget, as her mouth did things to him that made him believe that if he curled his toes any harder, they'd snap the hell off!

With Bashar on his back with his legs slightly bent, Cyn mounted him in the reverse cowgirl position facing away from him. She placed her hands on his muscular things to steady herself and grinded down on him as he pushed himself deeper inside her tight pussy that appeared resistant, but gave way to the friction from her kitchen.

"Cyn, I want you to moan louder for me," he ordered. "I need to hear how good I make you feel."

"Ooh, oh fuck! Hell yeah, your dick feels so, so, very good!" she panted.

"And you can have it anytime you want! This is your dick, all yours!"

"Give it to me, then. More, please give me some more, motherfucker!" she ordered.

"Motherfucker, huh? I'll show you what a motherfucker I am! I'm fucking your hot pussy all night!"

Bashar was close to coming and he wanted to experience looking at his wife's face when he nutted, which prompted him to change positions. There wasn't anything to match the look of desire in her face when he engulfed her with his love. He knelt down and leaned his body forward, while Cyn locked her legs around his waist and backside. He sucked on her right nipple, while squeezing the left one for a while. Their bodies moved rhythmically like a rocking chair as he furthered himself in to his wife, penetrating her slowly, until neither of them could take anymore, leaving Cyndarella drenched with her husband's generous load of love liquor deposited deep inside her.

THE COUPLE ENJOYED a gourmet meal of surf and turf on the yacht, after they had showered and changed back into their clothes to head down to dinner. Rosa had a tray of dark chocolate-covered strawberries that she said she'd take to the couples' room, which they accepted.

"I've got some really good news you're going to love."

"What's that?" Cyndarella asked her husband.

"Well, I had a call from Mack a couple of days ago, and he asked me for some ideas about Las Vegas."

"I'm listening."

"I hooked him up with a deal at the Bellagio. He married Octavia there last week."

"Get the fuck out of here!" Cyn shouted. "Did he, did he really?" she asked.

"Yes, woman! Whatever advice you gave her must have worked, because Mack came to me and asked for my input. People still talk about how much they loved our wedding. You know we put it together in less than a month."

Cyndarella began to cry tears of joy for her friend.

"Oh Cyn, babe, c'mon!" he said with assurance. "I thought that would make you happy. What's with the tears?"

"It does. Bashar, Octavia has been through so much! There's no other woman I can think of who's more deserving than she is. Thanks for helping Mack. You two seem to be really getting along well."

"It's respect amongst men. I'm my own man, but I'm proud to be a good husband, son and father, and friend on occasion when needed. Despite my parents' mistakes, those were strong qualities they passed onto us. I want to share it with our children."

"We'll pass it on to them," she spoke caringly. "Baz, everything is coming together with our friends. Sean and Denise, Vette and Louis, and now Tavie and Mack. We should have a big party."

"Woman, you are Chaldean by association," he joked. "You can throw a party at the drop of a hat!"

"I love spending your money!" she laughed.

Chapter Sixty-Six

Tavie and Mackenzie exchanged their vows once more in front of their friends and family at a private ceremony at the Wabeek Country Club. The school season had gotten underway successfully, though a bit stressfully, as they had an increase in the number of enrollees at the last minute, increasing the workload for the already overloaded teachers.

The couple went to each table to greet their guests, and it was quite remarkable to look out and see the familiar faces of people who truly wished them well. Tavie smiled at Mackenzie, and he gave her a kiss on her forehead.

"It's so nice that we can all be together for something festive, and not anything sad."

"I know what you mean."

The pair got out and danced to the live band. As Mrs. Dooley had promised, they could dance the night away, and she wasn't joking. The cover band blew everyone away. Denise and Sean were laughing out on the dance floor, as were the Worthys and Tara Vern and her new boyfriend, ironically Black as well. They'd been introduced by Louis, she recalled.

"Like mother like daughter, Tara?" Tavie sassed to Vette's mother, who grinned in response like the Cheshire Cat.

Vernon and Willa strutted their stuff in some of the ballroom dances that Tavie never learned how to do, and they were impressive, as were her parents.

Vette was counting the days to her wedding, though she'd had a little scare that derailed her.

"Corvette, you okay?" Louis asked his fiancée.

"Yes", she nodded her head. "We can leave if you're not up to this."

"I'm fine. I needed to get out."

Vette had suffered a miscarriage from an ectopic pregnancy that had happened to be fathered by her fiancé, Louis. She'd taken out her IUD to give her body a rest before trying a hormone-free one when it happened. Louis was so caring and loving with her; it made her feel worse worrying that she'd never bear a child with him. He agreed that if she got pregnant again, he'd be okay with it, but the doctor said she'd have a hard time conceiving because of her female problems and actually advised against it.

The festivities of the evening came to an end, and everyone embarked on to the next latest and greatest adventure.

"It was truly an amazing evening," Tavie said.

"It was, love, which is a good thing, for you never know what the future holds, and right now, what I want to hold is you," Mack said.

Epilogue

Cyndarella's life had never been pain-free. She basked in the fulfillment of family and friendship that life offered her. She'd spent a rigorous morning working at the office when her cellphone rang.

"Cyn." She heard her husband speak in a worried voice that concerned her.

"Bashar, what's wrong? How is Dad? Please tell me everything is all right" she said, as her father was having a stent put in this morning. Bashar had taken him in for the outpatient procedure because her mother was home sick with the 'flu.

"I don't want to alarm you, but honey, listen to me. I need you to get in the car and come down to the hospital, right away. Pete is picking up your mother. Baby, please come," he whispered in a solemn voice. "Don't ask any questions, just come."

"I'm on my way."

A very pregnant Denise was concerned for her friend as she'd half-listened in on the conversation and caught the tail end of it.

"Cyndarella! What is it?" But her friend didn't stop to inform her. She'd keep her phone close to her and hope for the best.

Tears ran down Cyndarella's face as she drove to the hospital. She prayed that her father would be fine. He was only going in for a small outpatient procedure. When Cyn got to the emergency room, she was greeted by her family and her father's cardiologist who had a grim expression on his face.

"No!" Cyndarella screamed, as she peeked in to Resuscitation and saw her father who had just passed away. Bashar wrestled to hold his wife who crumbled at his bedside and wept.

"Forty-five years we've been together, and now he's gone," her mother said in disbelief. "My husband's gone!" She collapsed in grief.

"Damn it! Why'd my daddy have to die?" Pete cried, as he tried to console his grief-stricken mother.

About the Author

Vina St. Fran, a confident and vibrant multicultural author, has quickly established herself as a mainstay in the literary world, despite being relatively new on the scene. Best known as the author of the captivating Amorous Trilogy series, she skillfully weaves contemporary romance and erotica romance into her mesmerizing tales, incorporating diverse cultures and perspectives. Ms. St. Fran, a native Michigander, embraces her multicultural background, infusing her stories with rich and vibrant representations of different communities. Residing in the Midwest with her family, she continues to break barriers and provide readers with multicultural narratives that resonate deeply. With her unique storytelling prowess, she captivates audiences from various backgrounds, leaving an indelible mark on the world of romance literature.